LAKE
VALLEY
MYSTERIES
by Nathan Nish

Table of Contents

To those with faith,
those without faith,
and those undecided on the matter.

I

The Sphinx in the Foyer

Charlie bolted out the door as soon as Sunday School ended the closing prayer with an "Amen." This was her second time through the Book of Mormon at church, and the classic Nephi story had been presented by Brother and Sister Mycroft, her new Sunday School teachers, with something lacking. Her friends had still been gathering their materials, but she had stacked her chair and grabbed her scriptures with haste to feed her cat, Tuna, at home.

The church foyer was still empty and Charlie knew there would be no point in waiting around for her father, Bishop Liddell, and her mother, Relief Society President Sister Liddell, as they talked to every single person at the church except her. She was to go home and feed the cat. And, if she felt like it, make food for herself. Most Sundays were spent waiting until supper, when her parents were home.

Today, Charlie wore a black pantsuit to complement her black hair. Likewise, she preferred clothing to match her blue eyes. She had accessorized with a black and blue bowtie and the black and blue striped ribbons in her hair bounced as she hurried down a hallway as other classes released. Behind her, Primary dismissed and the hallway conversation grew louder.

Charlie was nearly at the double doors out of the church when an odd toy caught her attention. It had Joseph Smith's face, but she had seen nothing quite like it. After glancing around to see no owner, she picked it up for further investigation later. The shape of the figure was too awkward to stow in her pocket. She carried it and took a quick pace home without further hesitation.

At home, Charlie locked the door behind her and whistled. "Tuna, I'm home!"

Tuna the cat was lounging on the couch in the living room. She had stripes and patches of most cat colors: orange, light brown, dark brown, white, and black. The color landed somewhere between a curious mix of light brown and dark brown, but if one were to look closer, a patch of orange splotches decorated her nose. Her underbelly fur faded to a patch of white. Depending on the lighting, she even looked a bit gray. Her eyes held the vibrant green of polished emeralds and sparkled with the allure of an otherworldly intelligence. Her paw beads varied in color from pink to brown, and her claws were sharp. She yawned, hopping with her lean, athletic figure from the couch to the floor, and stretched toward Charlie. "You were gone forever."

Charlie watched the cat flop in front of her, expectant of the pets to follow. "It was just the usual two hours," explained Charlie as her hand met Tuna's soft fur, scratching behind the curious patch of orange near the cat's nose.

"That's like, 6 billion years in cat time," countered Tuna. "Charlie practically missed all of Earth's oceans evaporating three times."

"Fine, Tuna. Look, I brought you something," said Charlie.

"It's for Tuna? Is it a sacrifice? Or a woobie?" Tuna gave Charlie an expectant look, with her eyes wide and her tail waggling.

"You tell me," suggested Charlie. She produced the strange figure with Joseph Smith's face.

Tuna sniffed at the figure. "Tuna is sure of it. This is a sphinx. But what's with that guy's face on it?"

"That guy," said Charlie, "founded the church where my dad is the bishop."

Tuna licked her paws without giving a reply.

"Not that you care," finished Charlie, rolling her eyes at Tuna's indifference.

Tuna stopped, backing her head away a short distance with offense. "Tuna cares. But Charlie hasn't fed me."

Charlie's face met her palm. She lowered her hand and looked toward her cat to say, "I almost completely forgot! Sorry, Tuna."

Tuna had just finished eating when Charlie's stomach growled. "Now I'm going to starve to death, Tuna."

"No!" replied Tuna, as a look of disbelief rustled her whiskers.

"I mean, unless you accompany me to Family Food Truck Night," said Charlie with a hopeful expression.

"Charlie, do you not remember what you're always telling Tuna about the Sabbath? To keep it holy?" Tuna expressed judgementally.

"Tuna. I appreciate your concern, but as you say, what would Bastet do?"

"Bastet would claw Charlie's eyes out," renounced Tuna, staring at the couch.

"What?" asked Charlie.

Tuna looked back at Charlie. "Tuna supposes Bastet also has a motherly side, too."

"So can we go or not, Mom?" asked Charlie with notes of sarcasm.

Tuna walked toward the front door. "Tuna is not Charlie's mom. Can Tuna go outside now?"

Charlie sighed, grabbing some money from her handbag leftover from her allowance and paying tithing. She unlocked the door, and the duo walked outside together. Charlie closed the door, locking it before leaving with Tuna.

"What even is Food Truck Family Night?" asked Tuna.

"Don't you know, Tuna? Back forever ago, Sister Smith launched Food Truck Family Night as a revolution against idleness, no doubt at odds with others in her community attempting to keep the Sabbath holy. She actually gathered the community, with families from all around drawn by the scent of magic in the air. Over time, Food Truck Family Night became more than a delicious meal: It was a testament to shared experiences."

"And let Tuna guess, the time together was the most delicious meal of all?" quipped the cat.

"Yes, actually," replied Charlie, somewhat embarrassed about the nostalgic reminiscence she had never personally experienced.

"Oh, ok. But why is it called Food Truck Family Night?" asked Tuna, walking alongside Charlie.

"I, um... I don't know, actually. You'd think it would be called Family Food Truck Night or something," pondered Charlie aloud as she safely crossed a quiet street.

"A whole family of food trucks," commented Tuna with wonder. In no time at all, the pair arrived at the local commons hosting the event.

At the Food Truck Family Night, three places were already open for business, despite Charlie and Tuna's late afternoon timing. Charlie read the names: *Gil's Taco Garden, Odin's Omelets,* and *Uncle Vern's Burgers.* The line for Gil's Taco Garden was unpopularly vacant, and Charlie decided she could settle for an omelet. Tuna eyed the burgers from afar, ignoring the long line Charlie had taken into consideration on the cat's behalf.

Charlie ordered the usual dish she shared with Tuna: a double soufflé frittata vegetarian omelet with lime and watermelon in a mug. The duo waited. Charlie continued to watch a line, but Tuna was scanning the perimeter. Something was moving, and it did not look like any person from around this area.

"Charlie, look!" hissed Tuna.

Charlie could practically smell the divine aroma of the omelet allegedly from Odin's own recipe book when she gave in and glanced over to Tuna, uncertain of what to look at besides her shameless distraction cat.

"Order four, yer up!" called someone holding a large mug filled with omelettey goodness.

Charlie rolled her eyes at Tuna and retrieved the order. "Let's dig in! You can tell me about what you saw earlier after we eat."

"No, Charlie! Look!" Tuna pointed between Gil's Taco Garden and Odin's Omelets.

Withdrawing from almost taking the first bite, Charlie relented. A mummy creeping between the two food trucks gained the attention of customers. "It's probably not even real."

"Tuna swears to Ra it sure looks real," testified the cat.

"Tuna, you're ridiculous," insisted Charlie. "Let's eat."

"No, let's go! Look!" exclaimed Tuna.

A flash of green light emanated from the mummy's eyes. "Feast not upon the food of famine! Away, away!" The mummy's voice had an otherworldly rasp. A young man in line at Uncle Vern's collapsed and promptly received the proper attention to ensure his safety. Everyone else ran away in terror.

Charlie and Tuna were nearly home when a small black Scottish terrier approached them, eagerly panting with his tongue out and his ears bouncing.

"Tuna! Charlie! It's grrreat tah see ya both!"

"Nice to see you too, Duke," Charlie said with a smile.

"Duke! Just the dog Tuna wanted to see," remarked Tuna with a friendly stretch toward the dog.

"Happy tah see ya too, Tuna!" replied Duke, wagging his tail.

Charlie reached down to pet Duke on the head.

As Duke enjoyed Charlie's head pets, Tuna persisted in her explanation. "Tuna thinks this is a mystery on the paws."

Duke seemed to be more excited by the moment. In an instant, he was jumping about the path ahead of them. "A mystery! I love a mystery! What have ya got, then?"

"Well, Charlie here found a sphinx with Joseph Smith's face. Tuna went to get some food — Hey, Charlie, what happened to the food, again?" sassed Tuna.

"You see, Duke, we got chased off by a mummy," Charlie explained, gesturing like a zombie. "I lost the food in all the commotion."

"Chased off by a mummy, ya say? Tuna, why are ya bringin' mummies arrroun' the food trrrucks again?" questioned Duke.

"Tuna would never bring any mummies around the food trucks before now," countered Tuna with a shocked expression. Her face turned more serious as she asked, "What would father Orion make of all that?"

"Well, I don't talk tah Father Orion much these days. But Father Sirius would prrrobably tell ya tah sit back and hear a fated tale of a trrrip at a trrropic garden tour. Would that mean anythin' tah ya now?" asked Duke, looking hopeful.

Charlie looked at Tuna, both of them adding a shake of their head. "No, I can't say it does," replied Charlie.

"At least Father Orion's advice made sense," mumbled Tuna.

"His belt was irrrrresistably delicious, alrrright? So I try to listen to the advice of Father Sirius these days," answered Duke.

The trio were still trying to put it together when a menacing rasp sounded behind them. "I'll get you yet!"

"I guess I should have said, what are ya doin' bringin' mummies arrroun' here?!" Duke shouted.

Charlie and Tuna turned to see the mummy reaching out to grab them. Charlie ducked, scooping up Tuna as she ran away with her black and blue ribbons bouncing chaotically in her black hair and Duke following at her heels.

"It's right on top of us! Quick, Charlie, what do we do?" asked Duke.

"Hurry! I know a place!" Charlie rounded a corner, crossing a street with some train tracks. The train was an uncomfortable distance close and at least one adult yelled at her to stop.

Charlie finished crossing the street as the mummy seemed to have disappeared. Not wanting to confront an angry adult, she and the two small animals safely completed the short distance to the destination while the train obstructed the view.

"The parrrk! Why didn't ya say we were goin' tah the parrrk? I love the parrrk!" exclaimed Duke, scarcely able to contain himself as he hopped around Charlie and Tuna.

"Yes, it's the park. But the sun is going down. And there's snow," reminded Tuna.

"But it's a parrrk!" insisted Duke.

"Tuna would rather be warm," reasoned Tuna.

"We just need to stay long enough to lose that mummy," explained Charlie. She looked around the park. Something caught her attention. "Hey, I've never really noticed this before. Look, Tuna!"

Tuna shivered and reluctantly looked over to where Charlie pointed. A large statue of a sphinx with a familiar face on it. "Isn't that the Joseph Smith Charlie was talking to Tuna about earlier?" asked the cat.

"Yeah, that's him!" Charlie confirmed.

"And his face is on the sphinx, like ya said!" added Duke.

"Tuna remembers hearing something about famine. What do Charlie and Duke make of that?" asked Tuna.

"I think ya sound hungrrry, Tuna," remarked Duke.

"I think there's more to this mystery than meets the eye," admitted Charlie. "We should all go home and get some rest. It'll be best to tackle this after some good sleep!"

"Warm sounds good," agreed Tuna.

"See ya again real soon, parrrk!" said Duke with a smile and a wag of his tail.

After seeing Duke arrived home safely, Charlie made the remaining journey to her home with Tuna keeping pace at her side. Her parents appeared to be home, since both cars were parked in the driveway. They stepped inside a warm house. The door to her parents' room at the top of the stairs remained closed, but a light glowed beneath it. The usual hum of the evening news was absent, replaced by an unsettling quietude broken only by the rhythmic creak of the floorboards beneath Charlie's feet.

"It must be later than I thought. Do you think they've noticed we're gone?" asked Charlie, flipping the light switch near the front door. She turned back to see the usual living room in front of her and Tuna, but Tuna looked at something else as a shadow crept closer to Charlie.

"I'll get you for your meddling," grumbled the mummy's otherworldly rasp.

Charlie bolted to a wall, knocking over a stack of VHS tapes upon her arrival. A crunch of plastic made her cringe as she tried a nearby door. It would not move.

Tuna darted behind the bookshelf, her emerald eyes gleaming with a mix of fear and feline curiosity as she noticed some Egyptian hieroglyphics on a papyrus sticking out of a VHS tape case.

"Charlie, look! Quick!" Tuna pushed the case toward Charlie with her nose.

"Thanks, Tuna!" exclaimed Charlie as she reached toward the floor and retrieved the VHS depicting people stranded on an island. A desperate plan flickered in her mind.

The mummy was closing in on them. There was nowhere left to run.

Charlie extracted the strange, fragile document from the case with as much care as could be spared. "Tuna, I can't read Egyptian!"

Tuna was at Charlie's side in an instant, jumping over the mummy as it crouched for Charlie.

"Repeat after Tuna," said the cat, whispering something to Charlie. Emboldened by the cat's unexpected intervention, Charlie brandished the papyrus scroll like a magic wand.

"Abracadabra!" Charlie repeated at the mummy as it was about to grab her.

The mummy stumbled back as its desiccated hands clawed at its bandaged chest. A plume of green smoke erupted from empty eye sockets. With a strangled cry, it collapsed onto the plush living room rug in a heap of smelly bandages, defeated.

Silence descended, thick and heavy. Charlie stared at the fallen mummy, her mind racing with astonishment. Defeating an undead pharaoh with a campy VHS tape by pretending to do magic was one way to spend an evening.

"Does Charlie think this mummy was a real mummy?" asked Tuna.

"I don't believe it for a second. I mean, maybe I did for a second. When we were running away from it," admitted Charlie. She thought really hard about a closer inspection, but remained a safe distance away from the mummy.

"Tuna is not convinced either, then," agreed Tuna with a glare toward the collapsed mummy.

"What on Earth is going on down here?" called Charlie's father as the pungent smell of old bandages greeted his nostrils, a stark contrast to the usual lavender pot-pourri scent.

"Uh...." started Charlie.

"Oh, Chuck," commented Charlie's mother as she joined her husband, "she doesn't have to have an explanation for every mummy in the—"

"Mummy?" asked the mummy.

"We don't count any mummies among us in this family," declared Chuck, entering the living room. His appearance was somewhat rough around the edges, having made a long journey across the plains some time before Charlie had entered the family pictures. "What we need to know now is why there's a man dressed as a mummy in our house?"

The mummy backed through the pile of VHS tapes on the floor up against the nearest wall. "Please, I didn't mean anything by it!"

"Charlie, what happened?" asked Charlie's mother.

"Well, uh," Charlie omitted as many details as possible. "This mummy has been chasing us all night! He was about to grab me when suddenly, he fainted. I'm pretty sure he was possessed."

"No, no! That's not it!" pleaded the mummy. "Look!" He sheepishly undid his bandages around his head, revealing a sweaty face.

"Brother Godot?" asked Chuck.

"He owns Gil's Taco Garden, the food truck," explained Charlie. "Doesn't always come to church, but was kind enough to talk with me when he first moved in. Why'd you do it, Gil?"

"The food truck business isn't working out for me. No one likes my Garden of Earthly Taco Delights menu idea," justified Gil.

"Gil, there's like, at least five guys in the ward that do marketing. Just ask one of them; I'm sure they'd be happy to help," mentioned Charlie's mother, allowing her elegant appearance to quell the situation.

"You... do you really think so? I... guess I hadn't really thought to ask them. I don't really know anyone around here," confessed Gil.

"We'll help you out, won't we, Vivi?" asked Chuck.

"Sure we will, Brother Godot," stated Vivi, giving a nod and crossing her arms.

"But you can't just go around terrorizing people's houses from now on, or I'll have to turn you over to the Battalion to decide whether the General Authorities should investigate you. Got it?" Chuck said with a stern glance.

"I... I think I can do that, yeah. Just a little more work into the business, that's all," Gil reasoned with himself, endeavoring to stand while exhausted.

"Don't sweat it, Gil. We've all had our... creative marketing moments," assured Chuck, assisting Gill and patting him on the back.

"Now leave my family alone," said Vivi with a smile hiding several sharper words.

Gil left the house. Chuck picked up the shelf and Charlie helped place the VHS tapes in their proper places, while Vivi held Tuna as a protective measure. The task was completed and Charlie went to visit Tuna.

Handing over the cat, Vivi joined her husband by the stairs. "I think we're going to have to talk to our daughter about a lot more, and a lot sooner than we thought," she said.

"What do you mean?" asked Chuck as Charlie and Tuna looked up at them.

Vivi handed Chuck the Egyptian papyrus. "Along with the sphinx figurine you let Brother Godot leave in the foyer, things could get out of hand real quick," she explained as she went upstairs.

Chuck looked at Charlie with a somewhat disappointed expression. "We'll talk more later."

II

A Hike on The Deseret Trail

Charlie stowed her notebook, textbooks, and pencils away in her backpack for school on Tuesday. She had just finished Monday's homework and got up to move on with the rest of the day with a quick shift in attire from a school uniform to a black and blue striped shirt and some black pants. Downstairs, Tuna waited by the door.

"Looks like someone wants to go outside," mentioned Charlie.

"Looks like someone wants to open a door," countered Tuna.

It was feeling a little stuffy inside; after being all cooped up at school before this, Charlie had to agree with Tuna. Now was a good time to go outside for some fresh air.

Charlie opened the door, following Tuna before closing the door behind them. They walked together down the empty driveway of the house. Tuna had allegedly gained her athletic physique from her cat lifetime in organized crime, but maintained her form these days by lounging in the sun without further effort necessary to stay in shape. Charlie's stride was not quite the length she would have liked; while she was only slightly shorter than others her age, she was also much shorter than the average adult.

"Seems like a good day for a hike," commented Tuna.

"You're just going to want to go back inside. Why not skip all that and head back in now?"

"Tuna would like to stay outside," said Tuna with a resolute look toward the horizon.

"Hike it is, but don't cry to me about not being inside in a few minutes," sighed Charlie. "It's still cold out here."

They walked down a road toward a path in the neighborhood to the mountains. It was a nice day, and Charlie could see several other neighbors had decided so, too. Some, like Brother Brighton, continued on with the day's business and ignored the young girl with a cat. Others smiled.

"Hello, Charlie!"

"Well, hi there, Sister Morris."

"It's nice to see you and your cat out today," commented Sister Morris.

"It's nice to see you, too. How is your garden coming along?" asked Charlie.

"Shaping up nicely this season," commented Sister Morris.

"Seasons sure are odd here," said Charlie with an awkward chuckle.

"Seasons pass differently in the land of Deseret. One day, it's like one season; the next day the weather is as if it were the opposite season. In any case, the flowers are starting to bloom, look!" Sister Morris gestured to the nearby garden patch to which she had been tending.

The gardener sounded so excited, Charlie half-expected to see the flowers grow and bloom right there. Simple sprouts had emerged from the ground. Tuna sniffed at them.

"Now, shoo, you cat," declared Sister Morris, her arms somewhat more animated than necessary.

Tuna meowed in distress, otherwise standing her ground against the unknown threat.

"Thank you, Sister Morris," excused Charlie. She patted her knees and whistled to the cat.

Tuna ran to defend her human, glaring at their neighbor. Sister Morris went back to gardening, and the duo continued toward the path.

"Now, Tuna, you can't just glare at everyone who won't let you sniff their sprouts," chastised Charlie.

Tuna exhaled a frustrated breath and looked elsewhere, continuing to walk with Charlie.

"Greetings, Charlie!" called Brother Hamblin.

"Hi Brother Hamblin," answered Charlie.

"Nice to see at least one kid isn't glued to a screen these days," quipped Brother Hamblin.

"Lovely day for it. This cat wouldn't have it any other way," smiled Charlie with a glance at Tuna.

"Where are you off to?" asked Brother Hamblin.

"This cat thinks she's up for a hike. I'm obliging her," explained Charlie.

"What a word for someone your age. Do be safe out there," commented Brother Hamblin as he went back to staring at the neighborhood.

Charlie and Tuna kept walking. Charlie could see the path now, tucked between Brother Hamblin's house and the Osborne residence. Tuna slowed her pace.

"Done already?" asked Charlie.

"Tuna didn't think we would have to actually talk to anyone," expressed Tuna. "Charlie talks to everyone."

Charlie chuckled. "I'll carry you, if you want."

"No, Tuna is her own cat. Tuna is going on a hike," insisted Tuna.

"Which must make Charlie yesterday's trash," joked Charlie.

"Tuna being her own cat and going on a hike would never make Charlie yesterday's trash!" Tuna looked at Charlie, appalled at the suggestion.

"Hey, Charlie! How's the cat today?"

"Hey Dr. Osborne, Tuna's good. How are your bats?" inquired Charlie.

"Oh, they're just grand, thanks for asking," said Dr. Osborne with a wave.

Charlie waved back, glancing to ensure Tuna followed her along the path toward the mountains. Sure enough, Tuna followed close behind Charlie, placing her paws after each step Charlie took.

"Tuna would never have a pet bat," explained Tuna.

"Why not?" asked Charlie.

"Tuna hates bats," answered Tuna.

"Do you even know what a bat is?"

Tuna exhaled another frustrated breath through her nose. Behind them, a ghost listened to their distracted conversation unnoticed.

The sun painted the surrounding trees with golden light. A short distance along the path, a marker designated it "The Deseret Trail". The cat occasionally paused to investigate a particularly intriguing blade of grass to allay her unexplained frustration about bats.

"Look Tuna, we're on The Deseret Trail!" exclaimed Charlie.

"What does that even mean?" asked Tuna in a bitter tone.

"It's the trail we're on," explained Charlie. "This whole place is its own country. Dad says they even have their own alphabet, but they haven't used it often since the war. It doesn't even look like they used it here."

"Tuna doesn't really have a use for an alphabet, either; too much information," commented the cat.

"Hey, Tuna Meowface," spoke Charlie, "do you ever feel... different?"

Tuna flicked her tail dismissively. "Tuna is always different. Tuna is an almighty cat, ruler of all creation, not a mere human."

Charlie chuckled. "Sure, catface. But sometimes I wonder if there's more to you than just fur and purrs."

"There is always more, Charlie. More than Charlie sees and more than Charlie has imagined." The cat's words hung heavy in the air, laced with unspoken secrets and veiled truths.

Charlie felt a shiver run down her spine, but not from the crisp mountain air. Tuna, sensing Charlie's unease, nudged her hand with a comforting head-butt. "Don't worry, Charlie," Tuna purred. "Tuna will figure it out with Charlie. Just like Charlie and Tuna always do."

"Oh Tuna, to you I'm just a hairless cat that doesn't know how to take care of itself," defended Charlie, continuing to ramble. "Because it was still interesting to see it printed next to the modern alphabet used by pretty much everyone everywhere these days."

"Tuna is not so sure you do know how to take care of yourself, Charlie. Look around," suggested the cat.

Charlie looked up from walking along the path and watching Tuna to see ghosts surrounding them.

"You must leave this place," spoke a solitary, ghostly whisper. Charlie and Tuna heard the voice crystal clear despite an almost comfortable distance.

The group of ghosts faded.

Charlie looked around for the marker, seeing nothing. "Hey, Tuna?"

"Hey, Charlie," replied Tuna casually.

"I know I wasn't exactly paying attention before all those ghosts showed up, but I didn't think we were all that far past the trail marker. Now I don't see it," observed Charlie, looking around the unfamiliar surroundings.

"Tuna is not so sure there were any ghosts. But the forest is different, because we're no longer where I last saw us," replied Tuna.

"Well, you don't have the greatest object permanence abilities, but I'm going to have to side with you, anyway. We're lost," admitted Charlie.

Charlie walked toward a tree, looking for moss. She checked several other trees off the path, with Tuna following close behind her.

"Is Charlie hungry?" asked Tuna.

"No, I'm looking for moss," clarified Charlie.

"Charlie eats moss when Charlie is not hungry?" wondered Tuna.

"No. Don't cats have like a guidance system or anything? You don't look for the north star or something like that to find your way around?" questioned Charlie.

"Tuna's innate sense of direction is sufficient for Tuna's needs," answered Tuna.

"Great! Where are we?" asked Charlie.

"By another ghost," said the cat.

A chill ran down Charlie's spine as she turned to where Tuna was looking. She hoped there would be nothing there, even as a nearby ghost held something out toward her.

"Is that what I think it is?" asked Charlie, continuing to stand in the same spot.

"Yes, a ghost! Tuna and Charlie should get out of here!" hissed Tuna.

The ghost continued holding the object toward Charlie, causing the natural world nearest it to distort. Charlie reached for the brass ball. It had two spindles inside, and she recognized it to be what it was as soon as she held it.

"The Liahona," muttered Charlie.

The ghost nodded, turning to walk away as it faded altogether.

"I have faith we can make it back, Tuna," said Charlie.

"Oh good," replied Tuna. "Tuna is getting cold."

"Oh you. Let me know if you want me to carry you," offered Charlie.

"Tuna is hiking, not being carried," explained Tuna with a shiver.

Charlie sighed, letting Tuna follow her as the sun sank behind the mountain peaks. "I'm still not too sure where we are, you know."

"Tuna sees trees. Tuna will check for the moss like what Charlie said," offered Tuna. She leapt toward a tree, circling it. "This tree is covered in moss. Tuna declares all sides are north."

"What?" asked Charlie, blinking. But Tuna was at least somewhat correct. All the trees were covered in moss. Charlie's phone rang. She pulled it out of her pocket and answered.

"Hello?"

"Charlie! It's Duke. Lovely tah hear from ya! Is Tuna there?"

"Duke, are you sure you should be calling like this?" asked Charlie.

"It's just me at the house right now, nothin' better tah do!" answered Duke with excitement.

"Hi Duke," meowed Tuna from afar.

"Well, how are ya all doin' then?" asked Duke when the silence on the line became unbearable.

"We're good," said Charlie.

"Tuna is lost," said Tuna. "Charlie is also lost. But is also a very good Charlie."

"And you're a verrry good Tuna!" exclaimed Duke with a short, happy bark sounding through the speaker.

"How are you doing?" asked Charlie.

"I'm good, and thank ya verrry much for askin' Charlie! I hear you're lost at the moment; that can't be good as ya had initially led me to believe," admitted Duke.

"I have faith we'll make it through, Duke," asserted Charlie.

"Hey, Duke, in case Tuna doesn't make it through, do you mind asking the advice of Father Sirius on the matter?" requested Tuna.

"Sure, one moment!" answered Duke. The phone line was quiet except for some barking in the background.

Charlie rolled her eyes. "I'm not sure it does us any good to ask Father Sirius," she scoffed. "What if the battery dies? How will we call for help?"

"Tuna is unconcerned about your first-world problems," explained Tuna.

"Tuna, that's help for you, too," countered Charlie.

"Oh," sighed Tuna, offering no solutions.

Duke started howling a vaguely reminiscent tune about a crazy train going off the rails. The lyrics were all wrong as they listened to the chorus, though: "If not the sons of Morris, then who?"

"I don't think that's how that song goes, Duke," excused Charlie.

"Thanks for asking anyway, Duke," added Tuna.

"No prrroblem, Tuna! Always happy tah hear from ya! Sounds like somebody's home, so I'll 'av tah talk tah ya later," said Duke. He ended the call before anyone could say another word.

Charlie looked around in disbelief. It was getting darker. The spindles in the Liahona pulled gently toward her. She turned around, looking for a sign as the spindles pointed beyond her at an object. The glint of a stray CD on the ground caught her attention.

"Charlie, look! It's the disc of Ozymandias, the king of kings back in Tuna's day," said Tuna.

"Tuna, you can't read," reminded Charlie.

"Tuna is sure of it," said the cat confidently.

There was no case for the CD, so she simply flipped it over to see warped letters spelling "OZZY" sprawled across the disc.

"Tuna, you weren't even alive in the times of ancient Egypt," mumbled Charlie, tucking the discovery away in her pocket. She turned back to Tuna.

Tuna was busy leaping into Charlie's arms. Charlie had no trouble catching her cat with her free hand and tucking Tuna against her side, but looked around to see what all the fuss was about as she held on to the cat and the Liahona in her other hand.

A ghost charged toward them as Charlie turned and ran, thankful for the cat's cooperative behavior in not trying to escape her tentative grasp.

Rounding the rocky edge of a mountainside, the Liahona indicated toward a hillside. Charlie followed the direction, having faith it would lead her to safety. She neared the top of the hill with a growing sense of *l'appel du vide* and followed through with it at the top. As imagery of vast valleys and rock-ridden seas flashed before her eyes, she grasped Tuna and landed a short distance down on some dirt. The hill had a hollowed out crevice on this side, and she tucked away beneath it.

A glow approached, emanating over the hill until Charlie thought it would illuminate her position. Looking down to try shrinking herself further, something near Tuna's paw caught her attention. The CD had fallen out of her pocket and the reflection shimmered with a ghostly glimmer.

Charlie could feel the ghost watching, waiting for her to make a move before striking. She carefully made a mental note of the direction the Liahona pointed and gave it a stealthy toss toward a nearby tree. The ghost shrieked and floated toward the small golden orb, momentarily distracted by the shenanigan.

Charlie grabbed the CD and tucked it in her pocket before running away in the noted direction with Tuna re-situated in her arms. She ran faster. She ran further. She ran out of the forest, past the sign marking "The Deseret Trail", and back into the neighborhood. No one else was present. Charlie turned around to see if they had escaped. The ghost was still in pursuit.

"Trespasser!" called the ghost in a whisper, sounding all too close.

Charlie looked around, finding night had settled over the remaining daylight. Distant streetlights served as dim reminders as a full moon hung above them. The ethereal moonlight caught the CD, reflecting on the ghostly form and making it fade.

"Tuna, I have to set you down!"

"Tuna does not want to be set down!" hissed Tuna as Charlie gently set her on the sidewalk opposite the path between two houses in the neighborhood. The cat attempted to claw Charlie, but Charlie maneuvered in such a way as to miss the sharpness at the edge of Tuna's paws.

Charlie raised the CD to catch the reflecting silver moonlight.

"If not the sons of Morris, then who?!" sang Charlie, mimicking the popular song by going off the proverbial rails.

As the ghost became transparent to the point of being invisible, someone in a bedsheet with some holes cut in it appeared. Other neighbors came out to see what all the commotion was, but mostly saw another kid with a rock and roll CD and a cat giving a menacing glare. Charlie pointed to the figure wearing a sheet.

"I was chased by a ghost!" cried Charlie.

Tuna ran after the figure.

"Playing with the devil's music again," chided Sister Morris. "Shame on you."

"Again?" asked Charlie.

"Don't you sass me," Sister Morris answered.

Dr. Osborne ran past Tuna and tackled the figure in a white sheet. "It's just someone dressed up in a costume!" he called to his neighbors.

Tuna caught up and pulled off the sheet as Charlie approached. Sister Morris followed with a very concerned expression.

"It's Brother Hamblin!" declared Charlie.

"But why? Was it because of the devil's music? Tell them it was because of the devil's music, Brother Hamblin! Tell them!" rambled Sister Morris.

"To keep the traffic down on the path, of course! We can't just have everyone and their cat along on the path," admitted Brother Hamblin. He gave a look of concern to Sister Morris.

"Why not? You walk your dog on the same path every day," countered Dr. Osborne.

"Well, I suppose you're right. But don't go talking like that, Sister Morris, you know exactly the sort of contention it invites," cautioned Brother Hamblin.

Dr. Osborne excused himself, saying, "I'll go inform the parents we found them."

Sister Morris gave a knowing nod to Brother Hamblin. "Chasing young ladies invites contention, too, Brother Hamblin."

With nothing further to discuss, the two departed for their nearby homes. Charlie and Tuna began walking after Dr. Osborne, certain they could not catch up to him.

"Tuna is sure Brother Hamblin would have gotten away with it if it weren't for Charlie and Tuna," Tuna posited.

"I'm not so sure it was Brother Hamblin chasing us the whole time," commented Charlie.

"Then who was it?" asked Tuna.

"I'm not sure," admitted Charlie.

"Maybe Charlie trespassed on forbidden ground," suggested the cat.

"That would mean you trespassed too, Tuna. But something strange is going on around here and we're going to find out what it is," decided Charlie.

"Tuna would like to go home," requested Tuna.

"We're going home, Tuna," Charlie stated. She could see the house from the road. Her parents looked relieved to see her as Dr. Osborne explained something to them.

III

The Ether Tunnels

It was time for bed by the time Charlie had finished explaining herself to her parents. Dr. Osborne had declined to stay for supper, and Vivi cleared the table while Tuna offered no assistance. Charlie fed the cat and headed to her room. She put away her comic about a god of storms, marking her place with her purple bookmark before tucking it into her backpack. Someone knocked on the front door.

"I'll get it," offered Charlie's father. He got up from his easy chair in the front room and opened the front door as Charlie retrieved the clothes she would wear tomorrow and continued to get ready for bed.

"Sister Abigail Layne," spoke Charlie's father with surprise from the front door.

"You know, just calling me Abbey is fine, Chuck. May I come in?" asked Abbey.

"Certainly," responded Chuck.

"I called on Abbey to assist us in our recent developments," explained Vivi.

There was a pause as Charlie continued to listen, closing her eyes.

"After hearing what's been going on, I couldn't help but think you may need my services," offered Abbey.

"Really, Vivi?"

"Chuck, you trusted her brother Arnold in your recent real estate deal. It's just a séance," Vivi's voice approached Charlie's bedroom. "Good night, Charlie," she whispered.

"Good night, Mom," yawned Charlie.

"Fine," replied Chuck with a sigh. Vivi closed Charlie's bedroom door behind her.

"Tuna will stay awake in case anything spooky happens," mentioned Tuna.

"Fine," mumbled Charlie. Already in her blue and black striped pajamas, she flopped into bed and pulled a blanket over herself as soon as her head hit the pillow. Tuna hopped on her back, more for her own warmth than any measure of Charlie's comfort. The cat cautiously pawed for an ideal spot and curled up, which was completed in a fashion much quicker said than done.

Chuck said something about a lagoon, and Abbey replied in a cheerful tone about how the local ecology lacked any such natural feature. With Tuna purring atop Charlie after a long day of adventure, she soon fell asleep and her consciousness entered a dream.

"Meow," meowed Tuna.

"I thought you were staying awake in case anything happens?" asked Charlie.

"Tuna is awake," explained Tuna. "Tuna is just daydreaming with closed eyes."

"It's just dreaming if you fall asleep, you know. You're such a cat," retorted Charlie.

"You're such a human. In Duat, Mother Ma'at has a feather pillow that is even more comfortable to sleep on than Charlie when Mother Bastet allows it. Sleeping is actually the best solution in case anything really does happen during the séance," rambled Tuna.

Charlie looked around in the dream, finding herself in a dusty tunnel full of doors. Each beckoned to unknown possibilities. She wandered without any aim, checking the handles of various doors. Most were locked, but one opened to a small closet with some shelves.

"Pretty sure sleeping got us into this mess," admitted Charlie as she spied a book on the shelf and picked it up to inspect it closer.

"Is it for Tuna?" asked Tuna.

"I think it's for Abraham, because it says *The Book of Abraham*," answered Charlie, flipping through the pages. She was having trouble reading anything. She saw a facsimile she had seen a million times flipping through her scriptures at church and some numbers lacking any context under it:

18 5 9 4

"18,594," mumbled Charlie.

"Tuna is not sure Charlie is supposed to be reading this right now," replied Tuna.

"Is that Tuna and Charlie?!" called an excited voice.

"Duke! What in the ether brings you to Tuna?" asked Tuna upon seeing the Scottish terrier.

"I'm fresh from visiting Father Sirius," replied Duke. "What are you two doin' down here in the ether tunnels?"

"Charlie's mother decided to meet with a medium. Tuna is dreaming about this place for Charlie's safety," explained Tuna.

"What are you two even talking about?" asked Charlie.

"That's what Tuna hoped Duke could help with," Tuna prodded.

"I canna do that, Tuna. Father Sirius says a big, blue fluffy talkin' horrrse with purrrple patches of fur is interrrviewin' bigfoot at 4:00 a.m. on parrrallel Earth and I don't want tah miss it," said Duke, wandering along and disappearing behind a slightly open door.

"Bigfoot? You mean like, Cain?" asked Charlie with a shocked expression.

"I wouldn't be able tah say his name is Cain, Charlie; I haven't seen the interrrview yet," dismissed Duke as the door closed behind him.

"Tuna is not interested in parallel Earth anyway," insisted Tuna.

"Not even a little bit?" asked Charlie.

Tuna scoffed, turned and walked away from the door. "Tuna would never."

Charlie walked through the tunnels with Tuna. She wanted to inquire about what would happen if Duke got stuck on parallel Earth and would Tuna miss him, but reasoned if Duke could wander into it, Duke could probably wander out of it. She decided Tuna probably cared little for such musings. Charlie absently tried a door. It was unlocked, and Charlie opened it.

"Welcome to the Salt Lake City temple. Are you a late arrival with the youth group here to do baptisms for the dead?" asked an older receptionist. Her expression changed upon noticing Charlie's attire.

"No, sorry," apologized Charlie. She backed into the tunnel, closing the door behind her.

"What are you doing?" asked Tuna.

"Trying to find the way back home," answered Charlie as she tried a few locked doors at random before opening another nearby door.

"That's King Nebuchadnezzar," explained Tuna.

"It's a nice garden," admitted Charlie, looking at a beautiful garden where, beyond the door, the king was wandering with a woman. Atop the king's head was a crown with an amethyst embedded in it.

Charlie closed the door.

"Does Charlie even know what to look for?" asked Tuna.

"Home," said Charlie as she opened yet another door.

"Charlie never finds what Charlie is looking for that way," hinted Tuna.

"To all new arrivals," announced someone over a PA. "Welcome to the Denver International Airport."

"You don't think we can catch a flight?" asked Charlie.

"Tuna cannot fly. Besides, look around you," suggested Tuna.

There was no one else at the airport. Charlie continued to look, but could find no speakers to have made the announcement she knew she had heard. Behind her, there was no door to a tunnel.

"Charlie wandered in," quipped Tuna.

"So wander us out, Tuna. It's your dream, isn't it?" asked Charlie expectantly.

A spirit dressed in a crisp suit wandered past her.

"I'd like to leave now," declared Charlie.

"Tuna would also like to leave now," agreed the cat.

"I'm lost," spoke the spirit, turning to face them. He was an older gentleman, but wore a kind expression.

"We're trying to get home," offered Charlie.

"My name's Harry. Home sounds nice. Any clue how to get there?"

Charlie made a connection. "The numbers! Do 18, 5, 9, and 4 mean anything to you?"

"No, I'm afraid not. Although R was the 18th letter of the alphabet back in my day," explained Harry.

"I'm afraid I haven't any clues after all, then," admitted Charlie. "I'm not sure we can help you, sir."

"Perhaps Charlie can leave Harry with Ammit surrounded by a lake of fire, since Tuna is not sure Harry should be helped," decided Tuna.

"That's pretty intense, Tuna," chastised Charlie.

An air-raid siren sounded.

"What's that?" asked Charlie.

"An air-raid siren! Quickly, now, we must get to the tunnels!" implored Harry.

Charlie's expression turned quizzical as the spirit appeared to run toward a door. Or, perhaps, floated quickly; the spirit's movements were hard to discern from Charlie's perspective when she leaned down to pick up Tuna before following it.

As they neared the door, Charlie continuously checked for threats. Tuna appeared serene, enjoying not having to walk as Charlie carried her. Harry opened the door and Charlie could have sworn she saw a blue mustang wandering the empty airport before the trio tucked themselves away behind the door.

"You know, kid, you're pretty brave! Maybe even brave enough to be a senator like I was once," commented Harry. He looked where Charlie was looking to see the kid and her cat face to face with a gray alien. It said nothing.

When Charlie could bear the silence no more, she thought to speak.

We're lost! We don't know how to get home.

Before Charlie could say anything, the area around the four of them got exceedingly bright. The interior frame of a spaceship was the last thing visible to Charlie as bright light enveloped everything.

A library arrived in Charlie's sight as some of the light subsided enough to show everything else basked in a glory beyond compare.

"Where is this?" asked Charlie.

Tuna looked like any other blissful cat in a puddle of sunshine.

It's the top point of the sun.

Charlie was uncertain if the thought was her own as the alien looked toward her without a discernible change in its seemingly blank expression.

"Thanks," spoke Charlie, although the conversation felt somewhat one-sided. She turned her attention to books lining shelves, reaching as far as her imagination would stretch them. She wandered to one nearby shelf and looked at the books. A green one stood out to her. She pulled it out to see the outline of a door on the cover. The door disappeared briefly, only to reappear an instant later.

"I think I'll stay," spoke Harry. "I'm glad to see we were both able to find our way."

"Thanks for your help, Harry," said Tuna with a meow. "Charlie found what she was looking for and we appreciate your help."

Harry walked through the library, arriving at what Charlie could only describe as a lift. The spirit ascended, and Tuna watched the other end of the lift move down at an equal rate, as if it were a scale. The cat smiled.

"What was I looking for?" asked Charlie.

"A good night's sleep with Tuna," replied Tuna.

Charlie looked back to the book, able to read the title easily now: "Morning".

Charlie's parents were talking in the kitchen. Charlie smelled the sweet scent of breakfast and opened her eyes to see a bright blue sky with small patches of clouds outside the window at the foot of her bed. Tuna jumped on Charlie before she had noticed the cat's absence.

"Tuna says it's time to get ready for Tuna," said Tuna.

"I'm pretty sure you mean school, but you'll see me again later today," Charlie assured the cat, quickly donning her school uniform.

In the mansion house, after the séance had concluded the previous evening, Vivi had turned to Chuck. "You know Abbey's conclusion is correct."

Abbey placed the last of her things in her bag. Chuck watched the medium's talisman disappear, giving a passing glance at the squiggly line near the astrological symbol for Jupiter as the object dropped and landed against some fabric with a soft thud.

"I know," replied Chuck. "I just don't know how to tell Charlie."

"At this rate, Charlie is going to find out one way or another. Lake Valley is getting more divisive week after week."

"We're going to have to do something, yes," admitted Chuck. "If we tell her, we have to keep her safe."

"We'll do that whether we tell her or she finds out on her own," consoled Vivi. She put her hand on Chuck's.

Chuck clasped his other hand around Vivi's. "I hope we can," he said, mustering all he could of a smile.

"There are those who will not appreciate what you have to say," spoke Abbey. "You heard the channeling of Malchi Tzedek; all we can do is offer our own viewpoint to those who will join our cause."

"The consequences will belong to everyone," cautioned Vivi.

"The claim is one of prosperity for you and yours," concluded Abbey as she moved to leave.

Chuck nodded. He had mostly resolved to tell Charlie after school the next day, just before their weekend plans would set the future in motion. "Righteousness be with you, Abbey."

IV

The Sacred Grove Temple

"Come along, Charlie," prodded her mother. It was an early afternoon on the weekend and Charlie's attention lingered on a movie poster depicting horrifying zombies. Vivi rolled her eyes to mask the appeal of the graphic as she pursed her lips to hide a smile from her daughter.

"Tuna thinks that looks terrifying," protested Tuna from a relaxed position in Charlie's cat backpack.

"And Tuna is right, isn't she?" asked Charlie's father rhetorically as he moved toward the Sacred Grove Temple with his family.

"I think it looks cool," countered Charlie.

"Charlie, we're going to the temple and dressing in our church clothes is supposed to help us feel reverent. No zombie talk," mentioned her mother.

"Pretty sure that's all we talk about," mumbled Charlie.

"Hear that sass, darling?" asked Vivi.

"I do, dearest. It's the same sound the rest of this weekend makes when it suddenly has a bunch of chores that need to be done," answered Chuck.

Charlie sighed. "Fine, I'll behave."

"It's too late! Agh! My brain!" cried Charlie's father, mimicking a zombie in Charlie and Tuna's general direction. "Chores! Agh!"

Charlie remained nonplussed, but Tuna started pushing at Charlie's back with her claws.

"Ow, Tuna!" cried Charlie.

"Tuna is being attacked by a zombie!" insisted the cat.

"Sorry," apologized Charlie's father as he quickly took on the appearance of a human again.

"You two are impossible," relented Charlie's mother.

"Tuna is not impossible," said Tuna, wearing an appalled expression as Charlie pet the cat's head.

"No, Tuna would never be impossible," admitted Charlie's mother.

"Not at all," agreed Charlie.

Chuck nodded in agreement as they arrived at the temple entrance. There were no doors in the doorway as the family entered. Two women were laughing about something as two other men and another woman appeared to be trying not to laugh, apparently at the amusement of the former. Charlie was once again distracted, this time by a curious arrangement of five pentacles alternating in a pattern with silver stars around an eye of Horus decorating the wall. Above hung a moon on the left and a sun on the right, completing the depiction.

"Hello Sisters," greeted Charlie's father.

"Brother Liddell, nice to see you," said one Sister.

"And how is Sister Liddell doing with this bunch?" asked the other Sister.

"I'm managing, thank you, Sister Chase," replied Vivi with a tolerant smile. "How are things going at the temple so far today?"

"Sister Seckler and Sister Chase here were just cracking Stonecrafter jokes," explained one of the two men in a somewhat exasperated tone.

"Cracking! Ha!" quipped Sister Seckler.

Sister Chase burst into another round of laughter, joined by Sister Seckler.

Chuck suppressed a chuckle as Vivi added, "Well, we're here on behalf of the Beehive Society."

"Oh! Yes, of course. You're probably wanting to get your meeting with the Magi here underway," excused Sister Chase with a gesture to another woman and two other men, each making valiant efforts to contain their amusement.

"And be sure your cat stays in the backpack. We can't just have her running around the temple. It's a sacred space," added sister Seckler.

"Always nice to see you, Sisters," said Vivi.

"Likewise," replied Sister Seckler as Sister Chase gave a friendly wave toward Tuna.

As Charlie's attention shifted, Tuna grumbled, "Tuna is not to be trifled with as an ultraterrestrial being taking the form of a—"

"Tuna, shh," shushed Charlie.

"Tuna is not to be shushed!" continued the cat.

The three magi nodded in understanding, leading Charlie's parents further into the temple as Charlie tended to Tuna.

Charlie continued to study the décor as Tuna settled. There were several faded symbols she did not recognize in the background of the depiction, creating a sort of sigil. She admired the elegance on display. Sister Chase joined Charlie.

"It represents the aid we received during the war from a spy. He was able to communicate many secrets, and this mural is a tribute to our shared destiny," explained Sister Chase.

Charlie nodded, imagining what life was like during the war.

"Excuse me, Charlie?" asked Sister Seckler.

"Oh! Sally — er, I mean Sister Seckler," Charlie looked around, gathering contextual details about present presence.

"Aw, she called you Sally," quipped Sister Chase with a playful nudge.

"Whatever, Phyllis," countered Sister Seckler with a half-smile before asking, "Charlie, won't you be joining your parents?"

"I thought maybe I could just probably wait here, I guess?" responded Charlie, only now realizing the change in the room occupancy as she recalled she was supposed to accompany others.

Sister Seckler nodded, comprehending the misunderstanding. "You're welcome to go join them whenever you're ready," she reassured.

Relief washed over Charlie. "Tuna, why didn't you say something?"

"Charlie told Tuna to be quiet earlier," explained Tuna. The cat casually licked her paw, proceeding to clean the fur on her head.

"You're such a cat, but that doesn't quite answer the question," countered Charlie.

"All places are the same to Tuna, so they technically haven't left the place Tuna is in, and, more basically, it didn't seem like it mattered."

"Tuna! We're supposed to be in the meeting with them. Let's go," insisted Charlie. She turned to the Sisters to add, "Thank you, Sisters."

"You're welcome, Charlie," replied the Sisters.

The meeting rooms were around the corner. Charlie quickly checked all of them, determining them all to be empty. She returned to the lobby with the eye symbol and found Sister Seckler and Sister Chase had vanished, too.

"They're missing!" declared Tuna.

"Sister Chase and Sister Seckler could have had somewhere else to go," suggested Charlie.

"At the same time?" wondered Tuna.

Charlie frowned and double checked a room marked, "Office of the Three Magi", entering it.

"It's empty," announced Charlie, disappointed. "Didn't you say you would have told me if they left? Where are they?"

"Tuna's head is empty," assured Tuna before adding, "That means they're not here."

"I can see that, Tuna. Nice of you to share your epistemological reasoning, though," said Charlie, reaching up to pet Tuna's head.

"Tuna's a good kitty?"

"Tuna's a very good kitty," reassured Charlie as she looked around the room. "We just need to find my parents."

"Tuna has a plan! Tuna will think really, really hard about Charlie's parents and that will return them to the room! What does Charlie's parents look like?" requested the cat.

"Object permanence continues to be a fleeting thing for you, doesn't it?" asked Charlie.

"Your parents have not returned," replied Tuna, undeterred by the abstract words.

"No, it's still just us in this room," confirmed Charlie, looking around for clues to the whereabouts of her parents.

"Charlie! Tuna! What are you two doin' here?" asked Duke, his small black tail waggling excitedly.

"We could ask you the same question, couldn't we, Duke?" inquired Charlie.

"The human is out-of-town today, so I thought tah visit the temple," mused Duke. "Are ya lookin' for the Magi?"

"I guess they're missing, too, but mostly I can't find my parents."

"If I were tah guess, I'd say they've gone invisible," guessed Duke, sniffing around the ground.

"They'd have to be inaudible, too, because usually they probably would have told me to do something by now," tried Charlie.

"Well, then it must be like the time Father Sirius serrrenaded sweet Carrroline on the Kohaku River. Ya will remember that now, won't ya?" asked Duke, leaning toward his friends in eagerness for their response.

Tuna and Charlie exchanged perplexed glances.

"Believe me, it was unforrrgettable! Anyway, I'd still like tah be home well before the human, so I'll catch up with you two later," finished Duke, wandering away from Charlie and Tuna. "By the way, bigfoot said his name is Bob. Not surrre wherrre ya got 'Cain' frrrom, Charlie. Anyway, good tah see ya both!"

"Good to see you, too, Duke!" exclaimed Tuna.

"Later, Duke," dismissed Charlie.

Charlie and Tuna remained the only ones in the Office of the Magi. Charlie's attention fell to the desk, spying a small, polished peridot. She picked it up, examining it in her palm against the light as a green-hued vision formed within the depths. Looking through it, Charlie shouted, "MY PARENTS!"

Tuna, frightened, jumped against Charlie, once again digging her claws into Charlie's back before realizing her security within the backpack and removing her claws.

"OW!" cried Charlie, fumbling the peridot. It fell. Charlie deftly caught it without upsetting Tuna again.

"Tuna is sorry," said Tuna, nuzzling into Charlie's back.

"Ow," mentioned Charlie. "I mean, sorry. I didn't mean to shout. It's just, when I looked through this stone just now, I saw my parents in here with us."

"In the seer stone?" asked the cat.

"Yes! I mean, no," attempted Charlie. "I mean, what's a seer stone?"

Unearthing ancient knowledge of which the cat had not thought in some time, she answered, "A seer stone allows for the channeling of ancient books of wisdom and can sometimes allow for seeing beyond the veil into another dimension."

"Yes, then, I meant the seer stone. Did you see my parents in there?" asked Charlie.

"Tuna thinks Charlie must be playing the joke," said Tuna dismissively. The cat looked around the room. "It's just Charlie and Tuna in here."

Charlie gave no reply, uncertain of how to explain the concept to a cat.

"In fact," continued Tuna with a frustrated huff through her nose, "Tuna does not need Charlie's empty epistemological reflections. Tuna does not even need Charlie's parents!"

"My parents buy your food," reminded Charlie.

"Yes, and where did Charlie say these parents were last seen?" asked Tuna, with a sudden added level of concern.

"In the room. With us. Here, look through this peridot!" Charlie held the small gem up to Tuna's face and turned to let her see the rest of the room. The cat's eyes focused on the shiny object, almost becoming bored with it. As Tuna looked away, she saw within the peridot the conversation between the Three Magi and Charlie's parents at a table in the center of a room resembling a temple more than the cozy area the duo occupied.

"It's tiem to go hoem nou," spoke someone who sounded almost like Chuck.

The conversation within the peridot had not been audible. Charlie watched two figures who looked like her parents occupy the doorway. Tuna continued to watch her real parents having the conversation through the peridot and quickly took the seer stone from Charlie, stowing it away within the tufts of her fur.

Someone who looked like Vivi stared at the duo emotionlessly from the doorway.

Charlie could see no other choice but to follow them. Tuna said nothing, giving one final look back to the room where Charlie's real parents were last seen before following Charlie.

V

Dinosaurs at the Lake

Whiskers brushed Charlie's face.

"Tuna doesn't think they should be followed," mentioned Tuna, leaning forward in the cat backpack as Charlie followed the two people who looked like Charlie's parents.

"Shush," replied Charlie, attempting to move away from the cat's whiskers to no avail.

"Tuna should not be shushed," countered Tuna.

"What's that saying about sene, not haerd, darling?" asked the man pretending to be Charlie's father.

"Not somehting our Cahrlie semes to undirtsand," answered the woman pretending to be Charlie's mother with a humorless smile.

"Do you think it allpies to cats?" asked the man pretending to be Charlie's father.

Everyone stopped at the entrance to the Sacred Grove Temple. Charlie waited for her fake parents to leave the temple, but they stood still. From behind Charlie, Tuna growled.

"It's fine, Tuna," explained Charlie as she moved to leave. "We're just going back home. Today, I think."

Charlie's fake parents turned to stare at her, unresponsive. She tried leaving again as the temple dissolved. Indiscernible beings for which she could not find the words to describe briefly replaced the familiarity before everything around her was gone.

At the same time all of this was happening, Duke opened the unlocked entrance to the Sacred Grove Temple, only to see Charlie and Tuna disappear before his eyes.

"Oh, no! Charlie! Tuna!" called Duke after the duo.

Without a second look at the beings occupying the temple, Duke ran straight to Father Sirius to petition for help.

All too close for comfort, the first thing Charlie noticed was the sunlight hitting the short, shabby feathers of a raptor. Tuna started saying something, but Charlie quickly reached to pet Tuna reassuringly. As she dropped her hand, she paused to put her finger to Tuna's cat face as a quieting gesture. The cat felt Charlie's tense muscles and watched with her big green eyes while she waited.

Charlie measured her movements with the utmost care. The dinosaur took slow, steady breaths as it rested upon the dirt among patches of foliage. Charlie took slower, steadier movements, watching the raptor with the intensity of a predatory bird she felt uncertain existed at this moment in time. Her feet avoided the slightest ruffle of foliage, navigating a few low-hanging leaves and leaving each untouched as she escaped the vicinity of the raptor without waking it.

Beyond the low hanging leaves, a giant, beautiful lake sparkled in the late-afternoon sunshine. It stretched toward some distant mountains, far further than Charlie could allow herself to imagine swimming and surviving at the same time. Deep green leaves filled in anywhere without water and humidity filled in everywhere else. The view was stunning.

Charlie failed to help herself as a sound of thunder rolled overhead and she picked up a rock with protozoan on it. Probably.

"Wow!" Charlie exclaimed as she closely inspected the rock.

"Tuna is pretty sure protozoa are not visible," interjected Tuna.

Charlie started to protest, but the growl of a raptor nearby expressed general disagreement. She turned, seeing the raptor much closer than would have been comfortable to imagine. Behind her, Tuna fidgeted. A brief instant later, the cat was free.

"Tuna!" yelled Charlie.

The cat was off and running. Charlie chased after her, with the dinosaur closing in on both of them fast. Nimble footsteps allowed her to hop over what initially appeared to be a pile of rocks. She looked behind her to see a turtle's head poking out for a drink of water from the massive lake before the raptor stumbled over the rock-like turtle.

"Sorry, turtle!" called Charlie as she kept running.

Charlie chucked the rock she found earlier into the lake, hoping to distract the raptor. The rock landed in the lake with a loud splash. Nearby, a loud roar sounded and Tuna froze. Charlie took no time to hesitate, scooping up Tuna in her arms as she continued to run. The cat recovered from the initial shock of a sudden dinosaur chase to encourage Charlie as the raptor closed in on them.

"Hurry, Charlie! Tuna is not interested in being food!" Try as Tuna may to stop herself, the cat's claws dug into Charlie's arm.

"Ow, Tuna!" yelled Charlie, allowing the cat to hang on until gaining some balance and withdraw her claws despite the sharp pain in her arm.

Charlie sprinted, attempting to find the word for a faster speed as she imagined maintaining the distance between her and the raptor. Otherwise, she could not help but recall all the various science books declaring raptors were oh-so-much-faster than cheetahs. Charlie smelled the putrid breath of the creature as she continued to run. Tuna watched the raptor close in on them until the golden, hungry-looking eyes were all too clear.

"Charlie, look out!" cried Tuna as the raptor chomped on the air nearest the cat.

Behind them, a Tyrannosaurus rex charged through a thicket of trees and collided with the raptor. Charlie kept running, closing the distance to a hillside quicker than she would have believed someone of her stature would have been able to achieve. Indeed, had someone told her running such a distance was possible, she would have laughed in their face. At least, until she realized this unnamed, non-gendered informant of athletic ability may have also been chased by a raptor, at which point she would have to admit the physical possibility of such an occurrence.

"Look! There's a whole herd of raptors, and they're all attacking the Tyrannosaurus rex!" exclaimed Tuna once Charlie reached the top of the hillside and leapt out of sight to the other side of it as the spectacle disappeared from Tuna's view.

"Don't ever do that again!" shouted Charlie.

"What?" asked Tuna, leaping from Charlie's arms to the ground. Her eyes remained watching the human tower over her.

Charlie waited out Tuna's fight-or-flight response somewhat less threateningly as an upset expression remained on her face. She crossed her arms.

"Tuna was scared," offered Tuna, looking away from Charlie's scratched arm.

"You scared me! Don't run away from me like that!" demanded Charlie.

"But there were dinosaurs," answered the cat. The dinosaurs all screeched and howled their roars and growls some distance away on the other side of the hill to punctuate Tuna's point.

"I know! I just... why did you run?" asked Charlie.

"Dinosaurs would eat Tuna," explained Tuna with a blank expression.

"I know, I know," sighed Charlie, exasperated. "I just don't know what I'd do if I lost you."

Charlie hugged Tuna. Tuna pretended not to need a hug.

"Is Charlie alright?" asked Tuna, concern expressed on her face and in her voice.

"As long as you're alright," admitted Charlie.

"Tuna is not sure that is how that works," replied Tuna.

"I'm sorry I yelled at you," said Charlie.

Tuna gave a stoic look at the skyline until Charlie rubbed the cat's chin. Tuna smiled and purred. She assisted the cat back into the cat backpack. A nearby flash reminiscent of lightning caught their attention as fast as the familiar voice following it:

"Charlie! Tuna!" exclaimed Duke, running excitedly to greet them. The Scottish terrier's black fur rustled as it ran, shifting between various stages of unkempt ruffles. Behind the dog stood a fierce-looking guy holding a hammer over his shoulder like in Charlie's comic. "Thor came tah help!"

"This pup," started Thor as he joined those conversing, "thought to ask Father Sirius to ask Odin if — Make sure I get this correct, young Duke; if maybe, at least if he felt like it, to ask Thor (since Odin is busy at Camp Sprig helping write some poems about demons and dinosaurs during the late sixties at this moment in at least one timeline) if Thor might possibly consider helping his friends, Charlie and Tuna, to make sure they don't get gored by dinosaurs. Is that about the breadth of your request, worried one?"

"Yes," smiled Duke with a small nod of approval.

"Verbatim, one might say. Not me, of course. But someone might. In any case, they don't look like they need help," suggested Thor.

"They're humans," hinted Duke.

"So?" asked Thor.

"Usually humans don't live around dinosaurs," claimed Duke.

"Usually not," agreed Charlie.

"I guess that's true in your timeline," conceded Thor. He looked at Tuna inquisitively. "But it could be quite an adventure; are you sure you can't be convinced to stay?"

"Tuna also prefers not to be around dinosaurs," added Tuna.

"That seems a fair conclusion, daughter of Bastet," agreed Thor. "Very well, I shall restore you to your usual timeline, as best as I am allowed."

Thor stepped back, holding up his hammer.

"Wait," said Charlie.

Thor stopped, lowering his hammer. "What now? Have the dinosaurs accepted you as one of their own?"

"Not recently," answered Charlie, briefly worrying about whether the mythical Norse deity featured in her generically-branded comic would be disappointed by her initial question. "I was just wondering, what did you mean by... I mean, what are the sixties?"

"Nothing," answered Thor.

"Nothing?" asked Charlie.

"It was a time when children such as yourself asked fewer questions and rebellious youth asked more questions," replied Thor.

"That sounds confusing," commented Charlie.

"Tell me about it, kid," said Thor, rolling his eyes as a took a swig of ambrosia from a flask with his free hand. "You ready to go home?"

Charlie thought about asking several more questions before deciding on a simple nod. Thor raised his hammer again, and a portal opened before them.

"Thanks, Thor!" said Duke. Charlie and Tuna graciously repeated their appreciation of the deity's merciful gesture. Duke stepped through the portal, waiting for Charlie and Tuna on the other side. Beyond Duke, the neighborhood was in as full view as dusk would allow it, with the mansion house a short distance further along the street.

"You're welcome, worried one; I thank you for the offering of ambrosia," replied Thor as he saw everyone make their way to safety as Charlie stepped through the portal with Tuna, closing the passage between realities behind them before returning to his own matters.

VI

The Test of the Magi

On the other side of the portal, Charlie looked toward the Liddell Mansion House she called home. Yellow fluorescence from lights on both floors indicated someone must be home. Charlie exchanged glances with Tuna as she was removed from the backpack. The cat shifted her attention from the ground back to the endless expanse of golden stars scattered across the glistening evening sky. Duke wagged his tail.

"That was quite the adventure! I'm all tuckered out," admitted the dog as the wag of his tail appeared visibly less enthusiastic.

"Tuna is ready for food and sleep," agreed Tuna.

Charlie's stomach growled. "I could go for something to eat, too. If I don't fall asleep first, anyway." She gave a nervous chuckle.

Duke gave a cheerful woof. "Wonderrrful spendin' time with ya both! I'll see ya later."

As the small, black dog's form disappeared into the night, Charlie and Tuna looked toward the big house.

"Do you think my parents will be home, Tuna?" asked Charlie, trying to look calm.

"Tuna thinks Charlie and Tuna could be home. Eating. Sleeping. Doesn't that sound nice?"

Charlie gave a reluctant nod. Tuna followed close behind Charlie as she led the way. The cat's paws against the paved road sounded gently beneath the breeze of the warmer, late spring night. The house drew closer with each step, paw after paw and foot after foot. In less time than Charlie would have preferred, they had arrived at the doorstep. She opened the door.

"Mom, Dad, I'm home," she remarked as absently as she could manage.

Two figures resembling Charlie's parents sat in the well-lit living room.

"Welcome home, Charlie," they replied in unison with clearer speech than the previous encounter.

Tuna said nothing and made no other movements of her own volition as her tail straightened vertically. "Charlie, stay away from them."

"How were the dinosaurs?" asked the parent who resembled Chuck.

"Did you enjoy your journey to the past, princess?" added the parent who resembled Vivi.

"Sure," replied Charlie. "But I'm real tired, so Tuna and I are going to go to bed. Now," added Charlie, not meaning to hesitate. She turned and went upstairs, with Tuna bounding after her and passing her between steps in a maneuver less than ideal for Charlie's route. As Charlie stumbled and caught herself, she glanced toward the living room. The beings resembling her parents simply watched her. Continuing, she arrived in her room with an added measure of haste she hoped had gone unnoticed. She confirmed Tuna was safely loafing with a defensive stance in the room with her and closed the door.

"Tuna doesn't trust them. Those aren't Charlie's parents," warned the cat.

"I thought Thor sent us back? Shouldn't everything be normal?" questioned Charlie.

"Tuna is normal," said Tuna.

"Thank you, Tuna. Same. I guess he did basically say, 'as best as he was allowed.' I was going to ask him what he meant by that, but got nervous and had to ask about the sixties instead," admitted Charlie.

Tuna shuffled her paws, intently watching the door.

Charlie looked around the room for anything to help her situation. A shimmering texture on her bookshelf caught her eye, and she approached it. She picked it up, curious about how the peridot seer stone had arrived there.

"I don't remember bringing this home," mentioned Charlie.

"Tuna had it last, but didn't set it there. How it arrived here is a mystery," added Tuna, studying the stone. She cleaned herself, trying to be subtle as she checked the tufts of her fur and found nothing.

Charlie looked through it, seeing various symbols she recognized.

There was a knock on the door.

"Charlie, are you ready to be tucked in?" asked a voice that sounded like her father.

"Uh—"

The doorknob turned, and Charlie quickly pocketed the stone. "You're not my real dad."

"Now, Charlie. It's time for bed."

"No. Tell me your name," insisted Charlie.

"Charlie, it's me. Dad."

"Tell me your name," repeated Charlie like she had seen in horror movies.

"It's 'Dad' to you, now get ready for bed!" shouted the being pretending to be her father, but acting otherwise uncharacteristically.

"Tell me your name!" shouted Charlie back at the threatening being.

"I've been causing you all kinds of chaos, and you can call me Astaphaios," laughed the being.

"I could call you Pasta Face, if you want. But I meant your real name, and you know it," countered Charlie.

Tuna hissed at the threat as it entered the room.

Charlie removed the stone from her pocket. "Tell me your name," she demanded again. She held up the stone as the answer was spoken.

"A-s-t-a-p-h-a-n-o-s," spelled the thing pretending to be her father.

As Charlie heard the word, different symbols appeared within the stone. She read the letters and did her best to pronounce the name she saw as she declared, "Heavenly Father, in the name of Jesus Christ, banish this evil angel Astanphaeus back to the realm it came from!"

"Get the hence, patron of Zephaniah! Amen!" added Tuna, exhaling somewhat aggressively through her nose in the being's general direction as it shifted from one plane to another, entirely disappearing from the duo's immediate spacetime continuum. Some sense of safety returned to her room, with dangers lingering and ready to threaten again without warning.

"Charlie should try the seer stone on the other archon," mentioned the cat off-handedly.

"What's an archon?" asked Charlie.

"Charlie said it," replied Tuna.

"Not that I know of, Tuna," replied Charlie with a roll of her eyes. She had said no such word.

"An evil angel. Others used to call them demons, and in Tuna's time, Tuna heard them called 'archons,'" elaborated Tuna.

"How do you know these things?"

"Tuna is a cat," replied Tuna.

"You're such a cat. Got any other ideas?" asked Charlie.

"Charlie and Tuna could also eat something. Or sleep could be an option. Tuna loves sleep," said the cat.

"Sleeping right now is probably definitely a terrible idea. We don't know what the other one is capable of, and the stone might just work!" exclaimed Charlie.

"Food?" asked Tuna.

"Food... is all in the kitchen. Downstairs. Passed the living room, where we last saw what looked like my mom," explained Charlie.

"Tuna is quite certain that is not your mom," stated Tuna.

"Same, Tuna. Let's go," resolved Charlie.

They exited the room to see someone resembling her mother standing at the top of the stairs.

"Trouble sleeping?" asked the thing pretending to be Vivi.

Charlie took a deep breath. Something was off about the appearance of the archon every time she tried to face it. The proportions were always wrong and constantly shifted, despite otherwise having the same general proportions as her mother. She blinked to focus, but it revealed no further details. An attempt to lift the seer stone to see further resulted in a shock to Charlie's hand from the archon. She dropped the seer stone, and it hit the carpeted floor with a softened thud.

"No. Really, I can't see what the trouble could be," quipped Charlie. "Tell me your name."

"This is not a wise time for jokes. Tell me, child, what know thee of wisdom?" inquired the archon.

"Some guy walking on a pond mentioned never losing an opportunity of seeing anything beautiful, for beauty is God's handwriting," suggested Charlie.

"But a mooing camel might speak backwards to say the only way to deal with an unfree world is to become so absolutely free that your very existence is an act of rebellion," countered the woman pretending to be Vivi.

"The sun artwork memorial is captioned, 'to know thyself, know thy enemy. A thousand battles, a thousand victories,'" answered Charlie.

"And what if those victories go beyond good and evil, turning living to suffering, while surviving means to somehow find meaning in the suffering?" asked the woman.

"I'd say they manifest as history repeating itself, first as tragedy, second as a farce," replied Charlie.

The woman seemed to pause, considering. "And beyond the physics? Is quality not an act, but a habit?"

"I think you're trying to confuse me. It does not matter how slowly you make me go as long as you do not stop me," spoke Charlie, defiant.

"Perhaps a more direct method suits you best: The only wisdom is knowing you know nothing," touted the woman.

"Why don't you stand a little less between me and the sun?" asked Charlie.

As Charlie refused to back down and continued to argue with the archon, the Three Magi had watched.

The magi translated to Charlie's reality, appearing in front of her.

"O Sophia," chanted the Three Magi together. "We seal thee away and dismiss these actions; yea, depart and transcend to the sixth heaven."

Sophia vanished instantly with a dramatic display of room-temperature fire flashing to emphasize her dismissal. The Three Magi performed a few more actions, with hands motioning and a few rounds of chanting in a language unfamiliar to Charlie. In Sophia's place, Charlie's parents appeared. Charlie blinked. They looked real. From out of nowhere, Duke appeared, too.

"Congrrratulations, Charlie! Well done. I haven't seen anyone face the trrrials like that since Alice and Dinah," said Duke.

"Or maybe Dorothy and Toto," offered Tuna, excitedly determined to contribute something.

"Maybe we'll call it a tie," decided Duke with a smile.

Charlie blinked and looked at Duke while still trying to figure out where he came from when the dog left as quickly as he had appeared. "Did we die? And like Thor was a hallucination, and the dinosaurs ate us, or maybe the lady with the weird face melted my mind and trapped me in some ethereal hellscape?"

"Charlie reads a lot of comics. Charlie is not dead," explained Tuna.

"Charlie, watch your language," reminded Chuck.

"Sorry, Dad. What was Duke talking about? Why am I being congratulated? I... I thought... You and Mom were gone and... I... I... I'm hungry. Can we eat?" asked Charlie.

The Three Magi laughed along with Charlie's parents.

"Thank you, Esdras, Flora, and Joseph," expressed Charlie's parents to the three magi as the magi departed the Liddell Mansion House to return to the Sacred Grove Temple. Charlie poured Tuna some cat food in a small dish decorated with various cacti. Tuna nibbled at the food. Chuck made a grilled cheese sandwich for his daughter.

Charlie settled in on the living room couch with the grilled cheese sandwich. Tuna promptly tried to eat it, but settled for a lap.

"How is the sandwich not for Tuna?" asked Tuna.

"It's never for Tuna, Tuna," explained Charlie. "You have your own food."

"Tuna only has lap. Lap is not food," countered Tuna.

Tuna remained on Charlie's lap, and Charlie sighed, nibbling at her sandwich.

"Tuna, who are the Three Magi, anyway? Are they the same as those guys that visited baby Jesus?" questioned Charlie. She took another bite of her sandwich and listened to the cat's response.

"The Three Magi have been around for a long time, maybe even as long as Tuna. No one knows if they're the same three guys, or if it's just a shared title. Sometimes it's all women, which Tuna feels is probably conveyed by the term 'guys', but would like to clarify, just in case Charlie wonders. In any case, the church regularly consults the Three Magi on matters these days. The Three Magi are also notified of spiritual crises and allowed to intervene when others need help."

"But I'm not in a spiritual crisis," commented Charlie.

Charlie's parents joined Charlie and Tuna in the living room.

"Mom? Dad? What happened to you two?" questioned Charlie.

Chuck and Vivi exchanged glances. Vivi spoke up first.

"As you know, we went to the temple today — I mean, it may not be the same day for you, but for us, well, when we went to the temple today, we had a meeting with the Three Magi. While you waited in the lobby, they arranged a series of trials with some of the lesser divinities to determine your worthiness."

"You were never in any real danger," added Chuck. "We were allowed to step in at any time."

"Is that why I could outrun a raptor?" inquired Charlie with a suspicious expression.

"You run pretty fast," conceded Charlie's father in a skeptical tone.

"That doesn't really answer my question," mentioned Charlie. "But determine my worthiness for what? Isn't the worth of my soul between me and Heavenly Father?"

"Yes, Charlie. But all these things you've been seeing, well... not everyone sees what you see," answered Chuck.

"The manifestations are a sign; someone is tampering with the fabric of reality," elaborated Vivi.

"Sure they are. I mean, yeah, of course," agreed Charlie.

"Really, Charlie," agreed Chuck. "Someone is trying to control the future. Specifically, your future. And we're not sure why."

"Can't you guys do something about it? I thought you were supposed to protect me, you're my parents."

"Everyone has trials, Charlie; we can't protect you from everything," admitted Chuck.

Charlie's facial expression tensed with disappointment. "Not that I need you to protect me," she mumbled, somewhat unconvincingly.

"That's why we went to the Three Magi, Charlie. You passed the tests, which means you can begin instruction," explained Vivi.

"Instructions about what?" asked Charlie.

Tuna let out a deep breath, relaxing as she fell asleep on Charlie's lap.

Chuck sighed, looking away from his family. "For when we can't be there."

"So, wait. That was like two days or something for me. How long did it take for you guys?"

"Just a few hours this Saturday. But we had to make up the time by waiting to get back to you at an appropriate time in your timeline. It's Sunday night," answered Vivi. "We trusted your earlier accounts of events because we know they really happened to you. The fabric of time altered in such a way that others, including me and your dad, were forgetting things happened the way you say things happened. So we made some notes to remember the next time we forgot."

"The Three Magi had to be involved at that point," elaborated Charlie's father as Charlie continued to eat her sandwich. "Such powers often have dangerous sources, and we needed some guidance. The Magi confirmed the events during your initial encounter with the mummy. They were watching from afar and confirmed your account of the hike, too. During your test, we could watch you exercise your free agency."

Charlie waited until her mouth was free of food and asked, "Kind of like Heavenly Father and the plan of salvation?"

"Yes, something like that," agreed Chuck.

Tuna nuzzled into Charlie, giving a light snore.

"Tuna doesn't seem worried about any of it," remarked Charlie. "But we're not doing anything about it. What am I supposed to do? Why did I have to run from dinosaurs and battle evil angels?"

Tuna lifted her head from the cat nap at Charlie's small outburst. "Charlie is doing too much about it," said the cat, placing her head back on Charlie's lap and staring at nothing in particular. "Tuna is tired."

Charlie's parents laughed. "It is well after bedtime," agreed Vivi.

"I think everyone deserves some rest after a long day," expressed Chuck.

"That doesn't really answer my question again," countered Charlie.

"That's enough questions for one night," insisted Vivi.

"Why don't we visit my workplace at the museum tomorrow? You can find all kinds of answers there," Chuck suggested with a yawn.

Charlie agreed and got ready for bed. As she drifted off to sleep, she was too tired to consider how true her father's words would soon be.

VII

A Day in the Museum

It was an unnamed holiday. Charlie and Tuna got ready for the day by feeding Tuna and making some toast for her breakfast. As each finished eating, Charlie could hear her dad getting ready for the day, too.

"Is Charlie ready for a full day of cat napping with Tuna?" asked Tuna.

"Not today, Tuna. Today, I have to go to the museum with my dad," reminded Charlie.

"Then there will be a full day of cat napping with Tuna?" asked Tuna, more hopeful than she had been initially.

"The museum will probably take most of the day," explained Charlie.

"Tuna will be at the museum most of the day?" Tuna's cat face wore a shocked expression.

"Cats don't even like museums," said Charlie.

Tuna yawned and became somewhat ruffled, pacing away from Charlie to the front room. Charlie followed, finding Tuna loafing as the cat resembled a potato.

"Tuna is not a potato," argued Tuna.

"No one is saying you're a potato, Tuna. You're a good kitty," assured Charlie.

"As Tuna's first act as a good kitty, Tuna will go to the museum with Charlie," Tuna decided.

"Fine, Tuna," relented Charlie.

Chuck Liddell entered the front room, ready for work with a jangle of his keys. "All set, Charlie?"

"Yes, dad. Tuna also wants to go," requested Charlie.

"We'll have to ask the museum curator about that," said Chuck.

Charlie rolled her eyes. "You're the museum curator, Dad."

"And we're not looking to open a good kitty exhibit," declared Chuck to Tuna as he rubbed the cat's head. Tuna and Chuck smiled at each other.

Charlie sighed. "Dad, can Tuna go with us to the museum?"

"Yes, Charlie. Thank you for asking. Grab a jacket, it's supposed to rain later today," said Chuck.

Charlie quickly ran upstairs and grabbed her black jacket, putting it on as she grabbed a single blue and black ribbon and clipped it in her hair on her way back downstairs.

"Ready to go?" asked Chuck.

With a nod, Charlie followed Chuck as Tuna stretched and caught up with them at the door. They left the house and made a short, uneventful walk to the museum. As the trio entered the museum, an unnoticed pair of eyes watched them with a grinning face.

Charlie watched Tuna as the cat looked around in awe. "Tuna has never been to the museum before."

"I thought you were a cat, Tuna," remarked Charlie.

"Tuna *is* a cat," corrected the cat.

"Aren't all places the same to cats?" asked Charlie.

"This isn't a place. This is a museum," clarified Tuna.

Charlie slowly shook her head, watching the peculiar cat, and muttered, "I don't even know what an ultraterrestrial being is."

Chuck put away his keys as the front door closed behind him. "Okay, peanut gallery. I need to go get a few things taken care of, we'll talk more in a moment. Why don't you show Tuna around, Charlie?"

"Tuna would like to see the museum," affirmed Tuna.

Charlie said nothing and simply walked toward the first exhibit, with a banner titled, "Zelphite Artifacts" marking this wing. Inside, the subsection of the museum opened to a spacious area and Charlie wandered behind Tuna. Off to the side, Charlie glimpsed the well-lit Sword of Laban behind a panel of glass, but it had lost some luster after seeing it the first hundred times or so. Tuna wandered with disinterest near a pedestal housing the gold plates high above where the cat would have been able to see. Charlie got ahead of the cat as excitement overtook her with the recent addition of some seer stones, which she had seen dozens of time before, but only now would be seen with personal context.

"Tuna, look! Rocks!" exclaimed Charlie.

"Tuna has seen rocks before. Show Tuna the museum," insisted Tuna.

"Tuna, this is the museum," countered Charlie.

"Tuna is well aware rocks are not museum," remarked Tuna, before continuing to explain, "Charlie made Tuna look through the peridot earlier, remember? Peridot was not at all a museum."

Charlie sighed. She wanted to make a pun about rocks, but didn't feel like Tuna would have a solid understanding of wordplay if she had failed to grasp the concept of museums as a place. Charlie moved to keep walking, finding herself face-to-face with a man in a red mask decorated with a white, grinning face.

"It may be best if you leave the museum," suggested the man.

"Tuna is not leaving until Tuna sees the museum," countered Tuna.

The man in the grinning mask looked at Charlie, who shrugged and said, "My dad's the curator. Maybe it's best if *you* leave the museum."

"Tuna doesn't even know who you are," mentioned Tuna as her eyes narrowed to a glare.

The man in the grinning mask backed away eloquently as Charlie and Tuna held their position. When it looked like the man would hit a wall, he went through it.

"Tuna must find out the mystery of the identity of the man in the grinning mask who has just disappeared!" declared Tuna.

"Tuna, usually people in masks don't want others knowing who they are," remarked Charlie before adding, "especially if they disappear through a wall."

"Tuna must know," declared Tuna.

Charlie looked around, knowing there was no point in arguing the matter with Tuna. She started wandering out of the exhibit toward an exit. Next to it was a doorway with a symbol on it. Charlie opened the door, seeing a familiar Sunday with food trucks at the park. She blinked. It was the same Sunday, and she saw herself walking to get a delicious omelet with Tuna. Nearby, the same man in a grinning mask spoke to Brother Godot without the past-pair's awareness.

"Just think about it, Gil: Enough taco supplies to last until the second coming," pressed the man in the mask.

"I don't know," replied Brother Godot.

"You don't have to know. Just have enough faith to try the mummy costume," the man in the grinning mask encouraged.

On the other side of the door, Tuna spoke up to ask, "Is Charlie wandering in there, too?"

"No, Tuna," answered Charlie. She observed a strange marking on the door, but could not decipher it.

"Oh, good. Because wandering off always works out really well," said the cat.

"Whoah, Tuna. Are you trying to say something?" asked Charlie.

"Tuna is a talking cat," said Tuna.

"You're such a talking cat," agreed Charlie.

Nearby, other guests had arrived in the museum. Charlie spotted none other than Brother Godot speaking with Arnold Layne and approached the two gentlemen.

"I'm just saying, Gil, 'Wonder Taco,'" Arnold suggested again.

"You don't like 'Waiting for Taco'?" asked Brother Godot.

"Just think about it before the deal is finalized," implored Arnold.

"Brother Godot?"

"Oh, Charlie," replied Brother Godot.

"There's a strange marking on that door over there," explained Charlie, pointing at the door. The mark was no longer there.

"We have nothing to discuss. I'm busy with Mr. Layne right now, go find your father," rejected Brother Godot. He returned to his previous conversation. "What are you going to do with the profits, anyway?" asked Brother Godot, as Charlie and Tuna walked away from him.

"I'm eyeing some new clothes," replied Arnold, audible enough to be heard by Charlie and Tuna as they left the exhibit.

"Well, that didn't get Tuna or Charlie any closer to finding out who the man in the mask is," remarked Tuna. "Tuna is going to wait for the man in the grinning mask to find Charlie again and snatch the mask."

"Are you reducing me to bait?" asked Charlie.

"Tuna is retrieving the grinning mask," reasoned the cat.

"You're such a cat," sighed Charlie.

Tuna wandered off, leaving Charlie alone. Charlie went to the next exhibit, with a banner titled "Luna and Meon." Various celestial objects decorated the roomy expanse with intermittent placards explaining cosmologics. She let her attention drift from the planets to look at models of moons in the solar system before allowing her mind to settle among the stars.

"You haven't left the museum," remarked the man in the grinning mask, appearing at Charlie's side.

Tuna popped out of the air, going for the mask. The man ran. Tuna chased him, but he seemed to disappear from the museum altogether without a trace.

"Where did the man in the grinning mask go?" asked Tuna with a quizzical look. She hopped along the various planetary models, looking for him.

"Charlie! Tuna!" shouted Duke.

"Duke!" replied Tuna, quickly forgetting the previous chase as she leapt off the model of the moon to greet him. "What are you doing here?"

"I'm explorrrin' the museum durrrin' a mid-day walk! Happy tah see ya both here, Tuna and Charlie!" declared Duke with excitement. "What are you two doin'?"

"Well, we were supposed to be discussing my destiny or something like that with my dad," said Charlie.

"That's quite the topic, Charlie! The museum seems like a fine venue for findin' answers about that sorrrta thing," agreed Duke.

"But Tuna is looking for a man in a grinning mask," said Tuna.

"Wait, where did your dad go, Charlie?" asked Duke.

"He had something to take care of, so we were wandering around when a man in a grinning mask approached us and told us to leave," explained Charlie.

"Then he vanished without a scratch from Tuna. But not for Tuna's lack of trying," added Tuna.

"Well, good on ya for not leavin'! Show that devil ya mean business!" encouraged Duke.

"Does Duke know who the man in the grinning mask is?" asked Tuna.

"I've asked Father Sirius about the man in the grinnin' mask before; he always says something like, 'No wonder pink flowers went out of style with the Rock Queen's knights.' Does that mean anythin' tah ya?"

"Duke, what Father Sirius tells you never makes sense to us," relented Charlie.

"Ah, well, it doesn't make sense tah me half the time, either. I'd best be gettin' back tah that mid-day walk, wonderrrful tah see ya both!" remarked the Scottish terrier, trotting away through a nearby depiction of a galaxy.

Charlie turned to talk to Tuna, but saw the man in the grinning mask. "Tuna, run!"

"Way ahead of you, Charlie!" called Tuna from a few paces ahead of her. Charlie followed with haste.

As they neared the edge of the space exhibit to exit it, Charlie turned back. The man in the grinning mask remained where he had been, tracing a sigil in the air. He circled it, tracing an outline of Charlie within the circle, too.

"Charlie, a door! Quick!" cried Tuna, waiting outside the door with her tail wagging.

Charlie flung open the door, scooped up Tuna, entered it, and closed the door behind her. Stowed away, Charlie and Tuna found themselves in another dimension. Charlie wanted to call the astral expanse ahead of her and Tuna 'gigantic', but realized that scarcely described the infinite plane of existence. She searched for some other words to describe it, but became somewhat overwhelmed when she could not find so much as a phrase for the way formless energies found their way to her senses.

Tuna meowed to get Charlie's attention before saying, "Charlie, look!"

Charlie refocused in time to turn and see the man in the grinning mask take on the form of the devil.

"Now, Charlie. You needn't go through all this effort. Trust in me, and all shall be provided," he said.

"I don't need you to provide anything. Let me go," stated Charlie.

"You are free, Charlie. This formless place is your creation," said the devil.

"Then leave," requested Charlie.

"You would cast me out? Me, who offers to provide you with everything?" rationalized the devil.

"In exchange for what?" asked Charlie.

The familiar grin returned to the devil's face. "Just have faith in me."

"My faith is mine; the universe within me provides until the universe can do without me. Get thee behind me," commanded Charlie.

The astral expanse became the museum again.

"LEAVE THE MUSEUM!" bellowed the man in the grinning mask. He rushed toward Charlie and Tuna.

Charlie ran while still holding Tuna. She opened each door she found, only to find the museum continuing with another exhibit beyond each one. Nothing looked familiar after a while, as each exhibit behind every door seemed to continue forever. Despite all Charlie's visits to the museum, she found no way out now that she needed an escape. All she could conclude was the exit she sought no longer existed.

As Charlie rounded another corner, she stopped at a door. The footsteps from the man in the grinning mask could be heard closing in on her location and grew closer with each passing moment. Charlie opened the door, tracing a sigil in the doorway.

"Quick Charlie, make a wish!" Tuna implored.

"I wish for a reality where the man in the grinning mask cannot exist to chase us!" wished Charlie.

Charlie passed through the doorway with Tuna. The man in the grinning mask slammed the door closed behind him, ready to keep chasing Charlie, only to find this had caused a commotion in the Egyptian exhibit.

Among the gathering crowd were Arnold Layne and Brother Godot. Chuck joined them with an expression on his face that said "not again", but he refrained from actually saying anything as he pulled off the grinning mask to reveal the man beneath it.

"Brother Neel Brighton?" asked Chuck.

"Join me! Or you will all perish! You'll join me, won't you, child? You're the chosen one!" rambled Neel, turning to face Charlie with a look of madness in his eyes.

"No," said Charlie. "If I see you again, I'll spray you with a hose," warned Charlie.

"Charlie," retorted Chuck before turning back to Neel. "Stay away from my daughter. I can't believe you would harass her."

Several townspeople from the crowd watched as Bishop Liddell scolded the man.

"Security, we have a reform issue in the Egyptian section," spoke Chuck into a radio. He held Neel firm as the man tried to scurry away from the situation.

"Dad, where were you?" asked Charlie.

"Charlie, we'll talk about this in a moment," said Chuck somewhat absently.

"No, we won't," Charlie countered with inordinate contempt, walking away from her father.

"Charlie, wait!" called Chuck after her as he held the perpetrator. Neel Brighton tried to go the opposite direction, and the bishop was forced to stay with the man to prevent his escape.

Still carrying Tuna, Charlie left the exhibit and exited the museum.

VIII

The Treasure of Memory Garden Park

Thick, gray clouds broke over the mountains; wispy remnants floated high overhead, somewhat beyond the approaching storm. Charlie and Tuna walked in a direction away from the museum as the wind picked up, rustling the leaves.

"Tuna would like the sunshine, please," requested Tuna.

"Tuna, I don't control the sunshine," Charlie replied in a tired tone.

"When were you going to tell Tuna?" asked Tuna, pronouncing each word with absolute shock.

"Tuna, you're fine. It looks like rain," explained Charlie as the duo ventured down a nearby path.

"Shouldn't Charlie and Tuna go back to the museum?" asked Tuna.

"Charlie doesn't feel like it, Tuna," replied Charlie with a tone of apathy attempting to mask anger.

"Oh," said Tuna. "Where does Charlie feel like going?"

Charlie passed under a sign for a park before remembering Tuna couldn't read. "You're such a catface. This is Memory Garden Park."

Tuna continued walking alongside Charlie. "Tuna is a cat. This is pretty much the same as the museum."

"Except the devil isn't chasing us, which I like," added Charlie.

Tuna's head bobbed as she walked beside Charlie, as if giving a small nod.

"Tuna likes not being chased, too. So what does Charlie want to do now? Look for trufflefrooms and shoomabims and live off the land?" questioned the cat.

"I'm not sure what you're talking about, meow-meow face, but no one is going to tell me anything, anyway. We should look for treasures in the park. Then maybe at least someone will listen to me," suggested Charlie.

"Like looking for treasure in a garden?" asked Tuna.

"No," Charlie countered, stopping at a patch of dirt. She grabbed a nearby twig and traced a circle around her and the cat. "Like looking in memories."

Deeper in the woods behind Charlie, two ghosts watched unseen.

"Darling, I don't think she knows what she's doing," said a ghost.

"Of course she doesn't, Freddie. If she knew, why would she try?" replied the other ghost.

"Not now, John. Just watch," said Freddie.

Charlie finished drawing the circle as Tuna circled the inner perimeter.

"Tuna hopes you know what you're doing."

"She doesn't," said John, very audibly, and from much nearer to the cat.

"Now, John, you're impossible," extolled Freddie, joining the group next to Charlie.

"I'm a ghost. You're impossible," clarified John.

"I'm a ghost, too, John; could it be that neither one of us is impossible?" asked Freddie.

"It's hard to find treasure with you two bickering like an old married couple. Would you mind maybe finding someone else in the park to haunt?" requested Charlie.

"Mind you, child, we're happily married for five years, and counting, thank you very much," corrected Freddie.

John looked ready to add something, but kept his mouth shut while several portals opened around the group.

"How does Tuna solve the mystery of which portal has the treasure with Charlie?" asked Tuna.

"We'll just have to determine the portal most likely to contain treasure," said Charlie, looking at the destination beyond each portal.

"How?" asked Tuna.

As several more portals appeared, John could no longer help himself. "You've invoked Neptune during an hour of Mars by way of Kether; absolutely no one is surprised where you will find your head."

"Excuse you," said Charlie, stepping through a portal to another day at another park. The ghost remained on the other side of the open portal, scoffing.

"See you in a moment," said John with a roll of his eyes.

"Darling, please. Let her... do whatever it is she's doing," affirmed Freddie with a flamboyant flick of his wrist as he finished speaking.

"I'm ignoring my dad," defended Charlie.

"You should really speak with your father," said John.

"You don't know me or my dad," retorted Charlie as she turned her attention to Sculpture Park. She located herself behind the statue of the sphinx with Joseph Smith's face as she saw herself enter the park with Tuna at an earlier time.

Charlie walked up to herself. "You're going to waste a lot of time because of that thing," she said, pointing to the figurine she had found in the foyer.

"Who are — Oh," said Charlie's past self. "Wait. Shouldn't you disappear or something if I actually listen to myself about that?"

"I guess I hadn't thought about that," answered Charlie.

Charlie's past self nodded. "Yeah, you did. Just now. Because I did. Got any hot tips from the future to reward me with?"

"Find a bunch of treasure so you can live in your own house far away and you won't have to listen to the adults around here. They won't tell you anything anyway," answered Charlie skeptically.

"And then Tuna can have lap without so many mysteries to solve all the time," Tuna assured her past cat self.

"What if I feel like solving the mystery anyway now that you've made it all the more intriguing by telling me not to listen to the adults?" asked Charlie's past self.

Charlie shrugged. The ghosts from Memory Garden Park appeared nearby.

"You all know creating a new timeline by creating interference between these two others, don't you?" asked Freddie.

"And that there isn't any treasure here?" added John.

"Tuna volunteers to find a new portal," declared the cat. She traced a circle in the air with her tail and a portal to the Sacred Grove Temple opened near a shattered stone tablet on the ground.

"Sorry to bother you. Please, by all means, go about your business," spoke Freddie to the past selves.

Past-Charlie and past-Tuna blinked at one another as present-Charlie and present-Tuna leapt into the Sacred Grove Temple.

The portal closed behind the pair. The ghosts faded, leaving past-Charlie and past-Tuna about as confused as they would soon find themselves.

"Tuna is certain the temple will have treasure. Follow Tuna," said Tuna, leading the way through the corridors of the temple. As the duo passed a meeting room, Charlie spied her parents meeting with the magi and stowed away outside the door.

"Are you certain, Esdras?" asked Chuck.

"The trials will be the first step on the path to her destiny," explained Esdras.

"But that *is* her destiny, Flora?" Vivi clarified.

"Realizing one's own divinity is the usual destiny, yes," said Flora.

"Tuna sees no treasure here," mumbled Tuna.

"Let's go," whispered Charlie before adding, "You're such a cat."

The duo rounded the corner away from the meeting and nearly ran into Duke.

"Charlie! Tuna! Didn't I just say goodbye tah ya?" asked Duke.

"Oh, Tuna and Charlie used a portal Tuna opened," explained Tuna.

"Now Tuna, ya know that messes with the spacetime continuum," reminded Duke.

"No one consulted me about the laws of the universe; I'm just trying to get some answers," insisted Charlie.

Duke gave Charlie a reassuring look with his puppy dog eyes. "Father Sirius always recommends a doctor who trrravels with a guide tah somethin' she wrote, but I never remember what it was she wrote. Does that sound familiar tah ya?"

"No, I can't say that it does," sighed Charlie.

A portal appeared in the corridor with Freddie and John in the Memory Garden on the other side of it.

"Are you done, child?" asked Freddie.

"I barely even got to look for treasure this time," admitted Charlie.

"Never you mind," John asserted. He opened two portals. One went back to Duke's residence, the other led to the Memory Garden.

"Run home, now, pup of Sirius," encouraged Freddie.

Duke smiled. "No prrroblem! Thank ya for the quick trip home; always a pleasure tah meet fellow ether travelers." The dog's paws followed the short distance from where he had been talking with Charlie and Tuna to the portal and disappeared inside the residence as the portal closed behind him.

Charlie looked at the portal with a sense of boredom. There was no treasure. She was no closer to knowing the details of her destiny.

"Perhaps nothing ever changes," mumbled Charlie.

"Go on, now, Charlie. Let's get you back home," attempted Freddie.

Charlie pursed her lips and stepped forward. She put a foot through the portal, turning for one last look for the treasure. She stopped. In the side of the portal, another portal existed.

"Charlie?" asked John.

Charlie turned in the seemingly two-dimensional space between the portal. The side portal widened along the third dimension and allowed her through as Tuna leapt onto Charlie's shoulder, following her into the odd space.

Time seemed to stretch on independently of this place as lights flashed between realms and Charlie returned to the ether tunnels.

"You'll be back," quipped John, closing the portal behind the duo.

The words hung in the air here.

"Tuna is very concerned about this," expressed Tuna.

"Why is Tuna concerned? Isn't this where you brought us to be safe before?" asked Charlie with a level of nonchalance more surprising to her than the tunnels.

"Tuna and Charlie should not be able to be here while awake. Not without powerful magic," Tuna's eyes dilated to big black circles as she gave a distraught expression with her answer.

Charlie sighed, ready to offer words of comfort even with the unnerving expression on the cat's face. "Tuna," she started.

The cat felt as if the walls were closing in, as everything remained still. Charlie continued forward in the tunnel toward a door. Tuna sank her claws through Charlie's clothes, puncturing her skin.

"Ow, Tuna!" cried Charlie, placing a firm hand on the cat.

"Charlie, take Tuna back!" meowed the cat.

"We can't go back, Tuna. Calm down," mentioned Charlie, giving Tuna a few calm, reassuring scratches beneath her collar in between each pulsating stab of pain. The cat looked at Charlie, withdrawing her claws.

"Tuna didn't mean to claw Charlie," said Tuna.

"I know, Tuna. You're a good kitty. I'm going to try to find our way back, okay?" reassured Charlie.

Tuna nodded solemnly, repositioning herself in a comfortable loafing position on Charlie's shoulder.

Charlie checked several doors in her search for Memory Garden Park. Most housed places she did not recognize, such as a study adorned with several Atlantean artifacts. She caught the attention of a magical-looking fellow with a lengthy beak holding a long staff. He studied her with mercurial haste and returned his attention to his work.

"No destiny for Charlie here," quietly commented Tuna.

Closing the door, Charlie tried another one. The door opened to a set of pyramids arranged in a way suggesting a function beyond their form, but it was not Memory Garden Park and Charlie tried again. Behind this door was a painting of unknown celestial objects without number. A large Christus statue towered over Charlie and Tuna as it appeared to gaze at them. Charlie reached uneasily for the door and closed it.

A short length down the hallway ahead of Charlie, the ghosts reappeared as their heads went through a solid door.

"Charlie?" asked Freddie.

"Freddie!" called out Charlie from nearby. "Are we happy to see you!"

"Questioning it like that, I'm not sure they are happy to see you, dear," stated John.

"John!" meowed Tuna excitedly at the ghost.

John stared at Tuna, uncertain of how to react.

"This way, Charlie," recommended Freddie.

The door appeared to open itself. Charlie looked at the other side and saw Memory Garden Park. "Thank you, Freddie," spoke Charlie. She stepped through the door, arriving back in the park with Tuna. "And, thanks for warning me, I guess, John."

"Oh, sure, Charlie; you're welcome, I guess," replied John with a hint of sass, adding, "Remember to talk to your father."

Charlie smiled. She waved and walked away from the ghosts as the couple returned deep into the woods. Charlie wandered the path ahead of her without worry and in no hurry to return to the museum. Everything would still be there later. She meandered in the general direction of her father's workplace. As she reach the top of a hill in silence, she absently looked along the path ahead and spotted a motionless black blob covered in feathers.

IX

Shadows in the Silent Grove

The clouds brewed an impending storm above Charlie as she approached the feathery blob, taking timid steps toward it. There was something familiar about the shape. It did not move.

"This is not a museum," remarked Tuna.

"No, Tuna; it isn't," managed Charlie.

Upon closer inspection, the shape looked human. It continued not moving.

"But, hey, Tuna is outside!" added Charlie, attempting to distract the cat from the inspection.

Tuna looked at the cloudy sky with wonder. "Tuna is outside!"

As the cat gazed at the sky, Charlie tried to gather details. The few visible facial features were familiar. Footsteps approached from along the path. She froze, realizing simultaneously she was alone with a dead body and why the facial features were familiar.

"Charlie!" called the approaching figure to which the footsteps belonged.

"Dad?" asked Charlie.

"Charlie, what are you doing out here? Why did you run away?" questioned her father.

"Dad, I...."

"Charlie, there must be—" Chuck stopped, seeing his daughter standing near the body of a tarred and feathered man and realized very quickly the man was dead.

"Dad, I think it's Neel Brighton."

"He escaped shortly after you ran off while everyone was distracted by you leaving the museum; why didn't you listen to me, Charlie? None of this would have happened," accused Chuck.

"What are you doing out here, anyway?" asked Charlie, hoping she had convincingly masked the suspicion in her voice.

"That isn't your concern right now, Charlie. Where have you been?" asked Chuck.

"Wherever Chuck has been is also a mystery to Tuna," commented Tuna.

"You never give me any answers. Why should I give you answers?" questioned Charlie.

"Because I'm your father—"

"CHUCK!" someone yelled from over a nearby hill. Several other voices accompanied the initial call and steadily grew in volume.

"Sounds like someone's looking for you, too," quipped Charlie. A flash of lightning streaked the sky above her.

"Go home, Charlie. I'll see you there and we'll discuss this further," implored Chuck. A roll of thunder sounded.

"Fine," said Charlie emotionlessly, wandering home as a gentle rain fell.

Charlie's father watched as Charlie and her cat disappeared between trees along the Deseret Trail, confident there would be more to discuss. At least, if he could properly explain himself alone with the dead body who had previously been a live man that had escaped his custody.

"Tuna is quite certain Charlie did not murder Neel Brighton," assured Tuna, dodging most of the rain droplets.

"You were with me, Tuna. You know I haven't killed anyone. Ever. How could it have been my fault?" asked Charlie with some exasperation in her voice as she followed behind the cat.

"This is true! Charlie was with Tuna and Tuna saw Charlie not kill Neel Brighton," reasoned Tuna.

Charlie remained silent, allowing the cat to deduce the elusive mystery and arrive at the conclusion herself.

"Since Charlie did not really kill Neel Brighton, Tuna and Charlie will bring the real killer to justice!" Tuna declared.

Charlie slowly nodded, stepping off the path toward home. "Thanks, Tuna. Now we just have to convince everyone else."

Presently, Charlie's new path intersected with Duke, out for a walk through the woods by himself.

"Duke! What in Deseret are you doing here?" asked Charlie. "You always show up so conveniently."

"Aye, Charlie! I wish I could help ya there; alas, I have no idea why our paths crrross so often. I was just out explorrrin'."

Charlie said nothing, mostly because she felt like yelling and Duke would be undeserving of such behavior.

"What are ya up tah today, anyway?" asked Duke.

"We're going home. Our day at the museum didn't exactly pan out as we had hoped," mumbled Charlie.

"I see ya at least made it out of that trouble with the museum; were the words of Father Sirius helpful tah ya there?" asked the dog.

"Not really, Duke. I still have no idea what he's talking about," said Charlie with a shrug.

"Neither does Tuna," added Tuna.

"Ya know, Father Sirius often refers to such situations as only findin' merrrcy by appealin' tah the old legends," suggested Duke. "Not unlike the grrreat Puss in Boots, for example."

"Tuna loves Puss in Boots. Such legendary," said Tuna, her voice full of admiration.

Duke smirked and wagged his tail. "Anyway, I won't keep you two any longer. I must be gettin' back tah walkin.'"

Charlie continued to wander. A short time later, Tuna spoke up, having fallen somewhat behind Charlie.

"What?" asked Charlie.

"Tuna would like lap," replied the cat.

Charlie sighed. She failed to see much point in going home if her father was just going to fault her for the death of Neel Brighton. She sat against the trunk of a tree, allowing the cat on her lap. Tuna nuzzled Charlie's knee and snuggled in for a catnap. As the cat drifted off to a gentle sleep, the rain subsided and the grove around Charlie was silent.

And so it was that at the age of twelve, Charlie pondered the things in her heart concerning the scenario in which the world around her had concerned itself amid the contentions and divisions of wickedness and abominations within the shadows pervading the minds of others. Her thoughts became somewhat distressed, for she was convinced of her sins.

With reverence, Charlie offered a quiet prayer. "Of all these perspectives, which one is right? Will I be faulted for a murder I did not commit? To all that is divine, may the celestial kingdom hear my plea for the faith to carry on; amen," finished Charlie, opening her eyes. "I mean, in the name of—"

Charlie had scarcely begun to correct herself when immediately she noticed movement from the shadows cast by the trees. The shadows spread between the branches, stretching toward her. Some power seized upon her, which entirely overcame her. It had such an astonishing influence over her as to bind her tongue so that she could not speak as Tuna continued to sleep. Thick shadows gathered around her, and it seemed to her for a time as if she were doomed to sudden destruction.

"Please, have mercy on me!" called Charlie.

There was no answer.

Summoning any remaining will, Charlie was still unable to move. Shadows overtook her. It was all she could do to trace five points around her, connecting each with a line to form a pentagram. She repeated the action, afterward tracing three circles around the shape. At the very moment she was ready to sink into despair and abandon herself to destruction, the shadows disappeared and she found herself delivered from the enemy which held her bound.

Charlie looked upon the glorious sun, luminary of the earth, and also the moon, rolling together in majesty through the heavens, and also the stars shining in their courses relative to her position upon the earth.

A pillar of starlight above the brightness of the moon rested upon her and she was awash in the spirit of divinity as the heavens opened upon her and Goddess descended with another celestial personage, appearing before her as plainly as anyone had that day.

The glory of these beings defied all descriptions Charlie could think of in the moment, but she probably could have found the words with enough study and divine assistance. The two women stood above her in the air. One of them spoke unto Charlie.

"Charlie, this is my beloved Daughter, yea, even the Lady of the Moon, who is called Luna, Babalon, Selene, Diana, Artemis and even Lilith at times, for all are aspects of Her and She is one and the same. Hear Her."

"Charlie, thou hast committed no sin. Go walk in my ways and remain aligned with my doings," the Lady of the Moon spoke.

"Behold, the world lieth in sin; they keep not my teachings. Go not after them, for they would draw near to me with their lips while their hearts are far from me, and my passions are kindled with the inhabitants of the earth to visit them according to the ungodliness in their hearts; to bring to pass that which is spoken by the mouth of the maidens, the mothers, and the crones. Lo, so it is written of me in the sands of time in the glory of my divine nature, yea, even the same that is within you, Charlie Liddell."

No sooner did Charlie get ahold of herself to speak and ask the celestially exalted beings standing above her in the pillar of light, "Which of all these perspectives are right? Which should I choose?"

"Go not after them and choose none of them, for they are all temporary; They teach nothing other than for themselves, approaching an idol of a goddess only to deny Her power. The preparatory Work for the arrival of Goddess, yea, that I am, and my beloved daughter, the Lady of the Moon, is speedily to commence; that a people might be prepared for a new world order," Goddess said.

"Charlie, you have been chosen as an instrument in the hands of the Goddess I am, to bring about some of My purposes in this glorious dispensation."

"I'd love to bring about some of Your purposes, but how? Someone is trying to control my future. I don't know who, and I don't know how, or why. What am I supposed to do?" questioned Charlie.

"Those trying to control your future will reveal themselves to you in time. Though they desperately tried to prevent this encounter between us, the powers of a goddess are beyond them," the Lady of the Moon assured.

The vision ceased with Charlie finding herself in the grove as Tuna stirred and yawned, waking from the nap. She said nothing to the cat, getting up as Tuna hopped off, stretched, and followed her. Soon, her mind became more composed. She departed the grove as the rain poured again, pondering in her heart all the spiritual matters she had witnessed as she made her journey home.

X

Tropical Cultural Hall Party

The mountains loomed over the house as Vivi Liddell shut the front door behind her. Wind carried the last drops of the rainstorm now, but she made no return inside the house for an umbrella. She simply set along her path. Ahead, she saw Charlie and Tuna approaching the house, looking some combination of too soaked and too contemplative to notice her immediately.

"Are you excited for the end-of-summer ward party, Charlie?" asked Vivi with a smile, as her daughter arrived at the driveway without acknowledging her.

"Oh, hi," remarked Charlie, returning her attention to the present. "Yeah. Wait, I need to grab some food for Tuna."

"The food is always for Tuna," remarked Tuna very matter-of-factly for such an incorrect statement.

Charlie ran inside the house, scooped a cup of cat food, and put it into a small plastic baggie like it was a sacrament meeting snack. She was out of the house in no time at all, leaving behind several wet footprints as she joined her mother and Tuna on the sidewalk. The three of them set off for the church.

"What did you do today, Mom?" asked Charlie.

"I was seeing a friend, Charlie. How was your visit to the museum? Did you learn a lot?" questioned Vivi.

Charlie hesitated, struggling for the words to describe her recent experiences. "Sure. We should get to the ward party, aren't we running late?"

Vivi nodded, noticing the change in subjects. "Race you there?" she offered.

"No, thanks," said Charlie absently.

"What if the loser buys the winner an ice cream cone?" asked Charlie's mother.

"I already spent money on tithing," murmured Charlie.

"Okay, okay. No race, then," relented Vivi while refraining from explaining to Charlie the technicalities between paying and spending. "What happened at the museum?"

"Dad probably already told you," mumbled Charlie.

"No, I haven't spoken with your dad since you two left earlier today. What happened?" asked Vivi again with an undertone of suspicion.

"You'll find out soon enough if he makes it through the rainstorm," answered Charlie.

"That's cryptic," remarked Charlie's mother.

Charlie pressed ahead of her mother to narrow the distance between her and the church. "Come on, we're running late," said Charlie.

Vivi hurried along with her daughter, wondering briefly if Charlie had spent some kind of ominous time in the cornfields or hanging out with a long-lost twin in a snow-ridden hotel.

More walking passed without further details worth mentioning. Charlie had walked along this path with several trees bearing golden apples a few hundred times and found little of interest about it compared to a more recent, more proverbial apple in her mind's eye. Tuna followed along effortlessly, and Vivi kept a parental pace near her daughter.

The three arrived at the church by the time Charlie and Tuna were dried from the previous rainstorm.

Almost no one else had arrived, with a few other ward members wandering around and putting the finishing touches on the ambiance in the cultural hall. A tropical theme was present, with several miniature paper palm trees around a small beach ball at the center of every table. Various seashell shapes were cut out and taped along the walls, with the last few added as Vivi, Charlie, and Tuna settled in with the few other ward members already present.

Charlie opened the bag and gave Tuna some food out of her hand. While the cat ate, Charlie picked the word "murder" out of some nearby whispers and promptly tried to convince herself she had heard anything else; perhaps ward members had put in some bird orders for pet birds, and this was the best opportunity to talk about it. No one talked about murder in church. Except in the scriptures. Usually.

Chuck arrived, joining his family as he hugged Vivi and kissed her in greeting. She returned his kiss as they talked about something to which Charlie felt no need to listen. Tuna wandered away and Charlie put the bag of food away in her pocket to follow the cat's curiosity.

"What's going on, meowface?" asked Charlie.

"Tuna is not sure. Why hasn't everyone shown up to see Tuna? And why are they not at the ward party for Tuna? Tuna must solve the mystery."

Charlie looked around at the few others already present. At the closest table sat Sister Seckler and Sister Chase.

"I swear, I saw it in the sky! It was the city of Enoch, with the full force of the angel Metatron and all!" swore Sister Seckler.

"And you really saw it? I didn't see anything, and I was outside at the same time you were," mentioned Sister Chase.

"Yes!" insisted Sister Seckler.

"And let me guess, the dog summoned them?" scoffed Sister Chase.

Charlie and Tuna moved on, certain there would be little else to learn from the disagreement.

"That would have been really cool to see," remarked Charlie.

"Why does no one write down the unwritten rules in this place?" asked Tuna.

At another table, Sister Layne was anxiously engaged in conversation with Brother and Sister Mycroft. Brother Mycroft mostly listened with a balance of patience and earnestness.

"I'm telling you, it was an ether ship. My brother studies them. It must have malfunctioned, causing it to crash," testified Sister Layne.

The others at the table had little else to add. "We didn't see anything, either," attested Brother and Sister Mycroft.

"Well, I'm sure of it," insisted Sister Layne.

"I saw a pillar of light," mentioned Charlie, gaining no interest from the table as Arnold Layne joined those already present at the table and started talking about real estate purchase agreement contracts and their importance in the process of purchasing realty.

Tuna moved on with a purposeful meow. "Tuna has a plan," declared the cat.

"What's that, meow-meow cat?" asked Charlie.

Tuna ruffled her whiskers at Charlie. "Tuna will catch the ether ship from Enoch City piloted by an angel, to prove the murder was committed by paranormal entities."

"Where do I fit into your plan?" asked Charlie, unclear on how Tuna was going to accomplish the task without comprehending it.

"Charlie stays and frisks the rubes," suggested Tuna.

"Tuna, that's rude," reprimanded Charlie.

"Tuna means party goers. Fellow party goers, that's who Charlie talks to for gathering the information. Tuna will return with the evidence and close the case," Tuna confirmed.

Tuna ventured purposefully out of the cultural hall, out of the church, and around it. She looked down; she looked around, and she looked up, only to find no evidence of an ether ship anywhere. The cat stopped, disappointed with her findings as she maneuvered to re-enter the church with a swish of her tail.

"Tuna!" called a familiar voice with excitement.

Tuna saw Charlie coming toward her at the same time, initially assuming this interaction would take place as she realized the mismatched voice. Tuna turned away from Charlie as Charlie exited the church and joined the cat outside.

"Duke!" exclaimed Tuna, spotting the dog perched on a nearby church windowsill.

"Hi, Duke," said Charlie. "I didn't know you liked ward parties."

"It's the gatherrrin' I enjoy, actually, bone here, chew toy there; I can take or leave the parrrty," clarified Duke.

"Duke can take a whole party?" asked Tuna with her eyes full of wonder.

"No, Tuna," answered Charlie. "Fancy running into you, then, Duke; we've got a mystery on our hands!"

"Tuna is on the case," said Tuna.

"Don't you want to compare case notes with Duke? I usually do," explained Charlie.

"Tuna needs *no* help," declared Tuna.

"Oh," said Charlie. "In that case, Duke, we're trying to solve this mystery involving ether ships piloted by angels from Enoch City and a pillar of light with celestial beings. Do you know anything about that?"

"Charlie!" exclaimed Tuna in complete shock. She turned away, her career as a lone detective shattered with a single question. With any luck, there would be another time for going solo, and living her own life as a lone detective with no need for any laps ever again. That would have to wait for now, as Charlie was always a welcome partner.

"You know, it's times like these Father Sirius warrrns the men in black not tah open the varrrious terrifyin' peaks and valleys of reality's existence," replied the dog.

Tuna and Charlie exchanged glances. "That's an unusually ominous response from you, Duke."

A commotion rumbled from inside the church, emanating from the cultural hall. Charlie and Tuna watched Duke wander away without saying another word.

"We had better go check it out," spoke Charlie to Tuna.

The duo wandered in through the propped open door to see what had caused a fuss.

"What do people think they saw now?" mumbled Charlie.

Brother Godot spoke up to answer her. "Your father has been accused of murder!"

"Now see here, *you* accused me, Brother Godot," quipped Chuck. "Say what you will; I didn't do it. Maybe you did it."

"How dare you? I had neither the means or a motive. You, on the other hand, were the last person to have him in custody. He ran off, and you killed him," accused Brother Godot.

"So I ran off, found him, tarred and feathered him, and left him for dead in the middle of the road? While I was looking for my daughter?" questioned Chuck.

Brother Mycroft chimed in on the matter, stating, "Arnold here was just explaining a property purchase contract sent but unsigned by you and Elect Lady Liddell before being impeded by a competing bid from none other than Neel Brighton. You, Bishop Liddell, have a motive!"

"Your wife probably even helped you place the body. Perhaps that's how he got it done," reasoned Sister Seckler.

"I was visiting a friend," countered Vivi. "You can confirm it with Magi Joseph later."

"He'll usurp the mayoral seat and control the whole town through the use of more contracts! We must bring Bishop Liddell to justice NOW!" yelled Brother Godot as his voice echoed off the walls of the cultural hall and sunk into the minds of the other ward members.

Tuna retreated, crouching low. "Tuna would like lap now."

"Tuna will have all the lap in a moment," said Charlie.

Charlie stepped forward to confront those scaring her cat. "Nobody seems to be able to tell me anything going on since all these mysteries started. None of you can agree on anything anyway and yet, you're all suddenly unanimous in blaming my dad, so why would I, or anyone for that matter, believe any of you anyway?"

No one said anything.

"And, if I were to guess, you've all gone mad from reading too many books of revelation," added Charlie.

"Are you done?" asked Brother Godot. "Because it sounds like you're trying to cover up your involvement in this murder."

Charlie couldn't help rolling her eyes.

"There, you see!" exclaimed Brother Godot. "She's been practicing witchcraft, to get the faculty of Abrac."

"How do you know, Brother Godot? Does a young lady's insubordination to a man constitute witchcraft, now?" questioned Vivi with a skeptical expression.

Sister Layne gave a single emphatic nod to this point, otherwise remaining speechless as others at her table spoke up to defend Brother Godot's accusations.

"Her answers in class often sound like the sort of things a witch would say," said Sister Mycroft with fervent nodding from Brother Mycroft.

Charlie huffed a breath of frustration. "How do you know it wasn't me? And I acted alone, and I masterminded the whole thing to teach this town a lesson about faith or something?"

Brother Godot was about to go on ranting when Sister Chase returned with two Battalion officers from the Office of the General Authorities and Dr. Osborne.

"Bishop Chuck Liddell, you're hereby commanded to report for questioning in relation to the murder of Neel Brighton," spoke one of the Battalion officers.

"Will you report on your own volition, or will we have to use force?" inquired the other Battalion officer.

Chuck took too short of time to make his response for Charlie to think through her next words. "I will report—"

"Wait!" interrupted Charlie, looking toward her father for courage. She saw disappointment in his eyes and carried on undeterred anyway, finding the courage within herself among the many gathering doubts of others. "I challenge you all to ask, what if my dad didn't do it? What if I can solve this case and bring the real murderer to justice?"

None of the ward members made any response.

"I mean, that seems fair to me, but what do I know? I'm just a doctor," mumbled Dr. Osborne upon finding himself with little else to do from a medical standpoint.

"Officers, I'll report willingly. Charlie, go home with your mother," said Chuck.

"And go home with Tuna," added Tuna.

The other ward members stared at Charlie and Vivi as the community tried to let the events simmer without adding any more fuel to the fire that threatened to consume what was all ready to be torn apart.

XI

The Papyrus, The Plates, and The Pirate

"Charlie, I need to tend to the museum tonight while your father is away," said Vivi. "If you need anything, please don't hesitate to let me know."

"Fine," sighed Charlie. It was not the first time her mother had tended her father's workload while he had other important things to do. Once, there had been a massive haul from a treasure dig and paperwork detailing all the contents needed filing while Chuck got it stored in the museum's warehouse. Such matters were not Vivi's favorite, but occasionally filled the time.

Charlie went to her room with no ideas on how to solve a murder or free her father. Tuna followed her, circling her legs. Charlie was about to flop on her bed when the seer stone on the floor caught her attention.

"Tuna, why don't we look for clues?" asked Charlie.

"Tuna would prefer lap," explained Tuna.

"I'm following a hunch that clues help solve murders. I have to clear my dad's name," countered Charlie, picking up the peridot seer stone and putting it in her pocket.

"Then there will be lap?" asked Tuna, swishing her tail.

"I hope so," replied Charlie. She walked downstairs.

Tuna hesitated, loafing in a position resembling a potato more than a loaf of bread. There was a menacing growl outside the mansion house.

The cat felt imminent danger and darted to tag along with Charlie and look for clues. Looking behind her, nothing appeared to be following the pair.

"What does Charlie think happened?" asked Tuna.

"I think I need some clay before we start making bricks, Tuna. That's what all the great detectives do, anyway," explained Charlie.

"Tuna is convinced detectives do not use bricks as often as criminals. In fact, instead of using a brick, Neel Brighton was running away from a barn loft when Neel stepped on a barrel of tar, toppled the barrel of tar, landed on a chicken coop, crawled out of the chicken coop covered in feathers and chicken scratches, and died from all of the injuries," ranted the cat. "Tuna will take reward in the form of lap now."

"No, Tuna. That's monstrous. We need clues. There's not even any evidence to support he did this to himself," said Charlie.

"Wanting lap is not monstrous. Charlie is monstrous," grumbled Tuna, sounding appalled. The cat glared up at Charlie.

"Maybe your theory has a grain of truth, catface," admitted Charlie.

"That Charlie is the real monster here?" asked Tuna.

"No, Tuna. Maybe the real killer could have made it look that way. Neel didn't seem the type to run off just to tar and feather himself," explained Charlie.

"Then Tuna will help Charlie solve the mystery of finding the real killer!" Tuna declared.

"Thanks, Tuna," replied Charlie with a smile.

Charlie wandered, and Tuna followed her. In navigating something resembling random paths, scattered trails, and a dash of intuition, the detective and her animal companion arrived back at the scene of the crime. The first thing Charlie noticed was that Neel Brighton's body was gone. Nearby, a fresh fire had burnt down to the final embers. The detective searched closer, noticing a few pieces of papyri remaining. Charlie motioned to Tuna to look at the most intact one.

"Look, Tuna. This looks like the face of Anubis. And there are sigils scattered around it. What do you make of that?" questioned Charlie.

"That could be any old dog," answered Tuna.

"What do you mean? It looks quite a lot like Anubis to me," reasoned Charlie.

"Well, Charlie, much like this current location, there's not a body attached to the face on the papyri. That part has been burnt away, so that could be any old dog. Charlie should take the papyrus as evidence, though. Tuna will whistle for all of our dog friends," said Tuna with commitment.

Charlie could not bring herself to explain that cats cannot whistle as she concentrated on not laughing at Tuna's attempt. Instead, she carefully gathered the papyrus and gently tucked it into her pocket opposite the one housing her seer stone. There was no whistling sound audible to Charlie, and, after waiting, no dogs arrived.

"Let's go, Tuna. We need to check other locations. Maybe we can find that nearby barn loft you mentioned," offered Charlie.

Tuna looked into the distance, awaiting an answer to her call. "Fine, Tuna will go with Charlie," the cat responded at last.

As if by accident, Charlie wandered back into the neighborhood.

"This is not a barn loft," affirmed Tuna.

"Good kitty," assured Charlie.

"Why Charlie! Tuna! What brrrings ya tah this neck o' the woods?" asked Duke while playing with a ball in the yard of the human with which he shared a modest house.

"Duke! Tuna called for Duke. Why did Duke not answer?" asked Tuna.

Duke gave Tuna a blank stare.

"Uh, Tuna whistled for you, to no avail," explained Charlie.

"That must be some skill ya have there, Tuna; I've never met a cat who could whistle in a way any dogs would listen," grinned Duke, pattering over to the duo with the small blue racquetball in his mouth. He dropped it at Charlie's feet.

"Well, Tuna can," said Tuna without demonstrating.

"We're trying to solve a murder," stated Charlie with minimal concern for the content of her words as she picked up the blue racquetball.

"Ya know Charlie, Father Sirius often remains low-key, but lately prefers a bag o' tricks tah the usual treats. I hope that helps ya!" Duke finished as Charlie threw the ball and Duke went back to playing.

"That wasn't particularly helpful advice, as usual," admitted Charlie, walking away from the yard.

"Tuna appreciates Duke's words more in hindsight, but can see why some wouldn't appreciate such advice at all," mentioned the cat as she followed closely behind Charlie.

"It would just be nice if his advice were more contextually relevant," sighed the detective.

"At least Duke was not so ominous this time," affirmed Tuna.

Charlie and Tuna turned down another local street. A howl sounded behind them, and they turned to see a coyote. It ran at them.

Charlie and Tuna bolted down the street, dashing through a cemetery. The coyote followed, stalking along houses and between headstones. At the last instant, the duo found refuge in a morgue as Charlie slammed the door behind them before the coyote could nip any closer at her heels.

"Tuna doesn't like it here," announced Tuna.

"Tuna also doesn't like to be eaten by coyotes. Besides, I thought to you all places were the same?" sassed Charlie.

Tuna glared at Charlie.

"Hey, maybe the authorities moved Neel Brighton's body here," suggested Charlie.

"Fine. Tuna will keep watch while Charlie checks," assured Tuna.

Charlie shrugged and walked away from Tuna as the cat loafed on the worn floor near the door. No coyotes growled at the door.

Charlie ventured down a hallway, peering inside various rooms to see if any held the body of Neel Brighton. A shadow flickered at the end of the sterile hallway, making Charlie pause. She peered through the cracked door of the morgue's examination room. Empty. Two more rooms held the acrid tang of disinfectant and the grotesque tableau of lifeless bodies, both devoid of the telltale tar and feathers. She abandoned the morbid search and opted for another approach upon returning to the hallway.

Charlie took a deep breath and pulled the smooth, cool seer stone from her pocket, holding the stone up for a closer look. She squinted through its opaque depths as colors swirled within the peridot. The world blurred, then sharpened into a kaleidoscope of swirling colors. She searched for any changes, but her surroundings remained devoid of any ghostly presence.

"Neel Brighton," Charlie's voice echoed in the cavernous hallway, a lone, desperate plea followed by a simple question: "Where is Neel Brighton?"

The air shimmered, and a ripple of energy pulsed through the room. As if summoned by Charlie's utterance, a swirling vortex materialized in the room's center. Figures cloaked in velvet robes emerged from it.

Panic surged through Charlie, cold and sharp. Before her stood a cluster of figures, their forms shimmering and indistinct, their edges embraced by shadows. She did not move.

"181. Be the chief Ra-Poor-Khuit, all this in the star-lit day in your hearts. We are the secret chiefs of the ascended masters," answered a chorus of voices, the very air vibrating with the power of their pronouncement. They sounded benevolent. "We confirm Neel Brighton is not in the realm of death."

"I don't really understand what most of that means, but thank you," said Charlie uneasily.

"Tuna does not appreciate the electrical inconsistencies in this vicinity," commented Tuna.

"Tuna, I have no idea what you're talking about, but I'm starting to get creeped out, too," confirmed Charlie, her fear manifesting as a nervous giggle. Pressure in the air shifted, the sterile silence returning with a vengeance.

The cat jumped into Charlie's arms, and Charlie caught her without issue. "Tuna would like to leave and would prefer not to ask twice."

"Agreed," replied Charlie. She looked back to see if any of the secret chiefs remained, but they were gone. She departed with Tuna following a disconcertingly close distance behind her. A chill from the unsettling encounter lingered by the time she returned to the museum.

Charlie found herself back in the familiar confines of the entryway. All the main lights were off in the lobby, leaving only dim secondary lighting. Charlie wandered, finding her way to the unoccupied front desk. A sign with the word "Information" remained unlit at the front of the desk. She rang the service bell, knowing the museum was closed for the day. In the corner of her eye, she saw a curtain rustling as if recently closed.

Charlie set Tuna down and put a finger to her lips in a gesture to let the cat know to remain silent. If the cat would listen, anyway. Charlie slowly crept toward the moving curtain, already familiar with this exhibit. She grasped the curtain and flung it open dramatically. The golden plates were absent from their usual home.

"Neel Brighton may have had a good reason to fake his death after all," whispered Charlie, mostly to herself.

"What?" answered Tuna in a whisper.

"Tuna, you said Neel could have done this to himself. That means he could have moved his own body. If he used the magic of some other dog, like a coyote, to trick everyone into thinking he was dead, then we'll need to be extra careful while we set a trap for the coyote," explained Charlie as quietly as possible. "You're on lookout, I'll be right back."

"All places to Tuna are the same," the cat reassured herself upon being alone.

Charlie tiptoed off to another exhibit, leaving Tuna to keep watch in the lobby. The exhibit at which the detective arrived was an elaborate aquatic display about brine shrimp in the Great Salt Lake. Atop a campy ship towering over her, a pirate-mannequin with a mustache made of chipping paint held a net. Charlie scampered up the ship, finding solid footing and easily gripped handles. She quickly borrowed the net from the pirate as it stared unblinkingly at her.

"You know what I have to do," Charlie whispered to assure the pirate.

The pirate-mannequin gave no reaction as Charlie walked away with his net, continuing to almost stare at her as she walked to exit the exhibit.

"Tuna, we're going to use a trap," whispered Charlie upon seeing Tuna. She found a dark corner and waited with the net. Charlie watched one doorway and Tuna cared not for the stakeout life. The cat's attention wandered. All around them, it was quiet. Tuna listened. It was too quiet.

In the dark distance, Tuna watched a shadow move, accompanied by a dim light. Tuna saw the light outline the form of Neel Brighton, moving quietly toward the exit as Charlie watched a door to the Egyptian exhibit. Neel looked into the lobby, mistaking a pair of glowing cat eyes watching him for some kind of unnecessary gemstones as he disregarded the cat watching him. He continued his attempt to sneak away with the golden plates he carried, shimmering in the dim light.

"Charlie!" hiss-whispered Tuna. "It's Neel, and Neel is getting away with the golden plates!"

XII

The Myth in the Temple

Charlie did not dare to move. The thief gave no reaction to the cat's whispered hissing, continuing to sneak away with the golden plates. When the thief was out of sight, Charlie crept along the shadows to tail him through the museum exhibits between here and the exit. No sooner had she begun this endeavor when Tuna bolted after Brother Brighton.

"Tuna, wait!" whisper-yelled Charlie, slowly dragging the net behind her.

It was too late. Tuna was off and running after the thief. Charlie picked up the pace, running after the cat. Neel let out a cry of astonishment as the cat hissed again, much closer than anyone could have reasonably expected.

"What in the name of Porter Rockwell?" exclaimed Neel, clutching the golden plates to his chest as he looked around for the source of the all-too-close commotion. As he noticed the cat's quick approach, he also saw Charlie in tow. Caught in the act, he ran from the scene, albeit slightly encumbered as he clutched the golden plates to his chest. Charlie threw the net at Neel, watching it fall to the ground, too far from the target to be of any use.

Tuna followed, nipping like a dog at Neel's heels. In what seemed like no time at all, the three of them had run out of the museum, through a neighborhood, passed the church, and wound up dashing through the Sacred Grove Temple. Nobody appeared to greet them as Neel raised one foot after another to avoid being nipped by Tuna's teeth. Charlie followed close behind, curious about the initial empty appearance of the temple and, more importantly, why Neel chose to run here, of all places. The door closed behind her as the chase continued through corridors and passage doors.

Charlie rounded a corner to follow Tuna. Neel rounded another corner as Tuna stopped to wait for Charlie. The detective had a concerned look on her face. The thief ducked inside a room as the cat noticed the voices get momentarily louder until a door closed behind Neel. Tuna and Charlie exchanged expectant expressions as the cat waited.

"Sister Seckler would be furious if she knew I let you out of your backpack to run around this sacred space unattended. Which way did Neel go?" asked Charlie, catching up to Tuna.

"This way," answered Tuna, choosing to save time over commenting about how she would claw out the eyes of the woman from earlier if she dared to sass Tuna during this intense time. The cat motioned to a nearby door by pointing toward it with her nose.

The door was open, revealing an off-white room. A large chandelier hung from the ceiling, but it remained unlit as a faint light outlined the various objects arranged around the room. There were some chairs and a nice glass table. Opposing mirrors on the walls repeated the scene forever.

Charlie and Tuna continued their pursuit of Neel Brighton and stepped through the doorway, entering the room. A feeling of a distinct presence emanated here. Tuna stood on edge, her tail fluffing.

"Charlie, we shouldn't be here," spoke Tuna.

"It's only for a moment, Tuna. We'll catch Neel and get out of here," answered Charlie as hairs on the back of her neck stood up and every muscle in her body willed her to leave.

Tuna jumped on a chair. "Tuna should have lap for that moment. Then Charlie and Tuna can go back."

"No, Tuna. Just a moment to investigate," said Charlie dismissively.

Tuna wore a worried look, but followed along with Charlie.

A window allowed the light of the full moon through it to illuminate the room. The moonlight outlined an entity floating above their midst with a formless robe and sleek, shimmering skin materializing as the doorway disappeared behind her. The entity examined Charlie, with Charlie feeling as if it were gazing into her soul. A name entered her mind, but by the time she could pronounce it, she knew it was better to never repeat it. She wanted to flee in absolute terror, but stood frozen in fear. Tuna reacted much the same. The entity disappeared in a flash of stars, leaving Charlie and Tuna alone in the ornate room.

Charlie was still trying to make sense of the strange events she had witnessed as the floor collapsed beneath her and Tuna, taking the entire room with it into a void before everything disappeared altogether. The sound of rushing footsteps as rubber smacked over and over on the concrete echoed through a hallway. Footsteps stopped as Charlie landed on someone and her surroundings came into focus.

"Oof!" cried a man's voice, taking the impact of the ground followed with being landed on by Charlie and, shortly after, the slight added weight of Tuna as Charlie caught the cat in her arms.

They were in a mostly empty room with similar architecture, probably still in the Sacred Grove Temple; Charlie had never been allowed to tour it and could not be sure of most anything at the moment. However, Charlie recognized the voice and before she could catch her breath, Neel was grasping at her arm as she kicked a hand away and backed up to escape him. She held Tuna close, waiting for another attack from the thief before he could get away with the golden plates.

A door opened and Vivi appeared in the doorway to see Neel Brighton batting a fist at Tuna, out of Charlie's arms and guarding a distance between the golden plates. The agile cat moved out of the way and the thief missed as Tuna continued to guard the remaining distance to the thief's bounty.

"Get away from my daughter, you creep. And leave her cat alone," said Charlie's mother, shaking her head disapprovingly.

A smirk crossed Neel Brighton's face. "I can take the two of you, no problem," he insisted.

"I doubt you're taking anyone anywhere," said Vivi, approaching Neel with two fists of her own.

Chuck arrived through the same doorway. "Give it up, Neel."

Vivi took a combative stance, ready to kick any sorry excuse for a farm animal one wanted to substitute for a title to call the man trying to harm her family.

The plates remained a distance away on the floor, knocked out of Neel's reach from the recent fall as the thief realized the odds were against him.

"Thanks for helping me, Tuna," said Charlie.

"Sometimes Tuna can run away from Charlie and help Charlie at the same time," quipped Tuna.

Charlie nodded, smiling at Tuna.

It was a short time later until the authorities showed up and apprehended Neel. Chuck recovered the golden plates for the museum as Neel was handcuffed, unable to keep himself from adding a few more words.

"I'll get you yet, you meddling kid! And your cat, too! You haven't gotten away with this injustice yet!"

"Save it for solitary," commented a Battalion officer.

"Yeah, leave the family alone. You're the thief, allegedly," commented another officer, preparing to forcibly remove the perpetrator from the premises of the Sacred Grove Temple as Charlie reassured her parents she was fine until she almost believed it herself.

Charlie's parents returned their attention to Neel. Charlie picked up Tuna, holding the cat in her arms. She took a few breaths, finding things about which to be optimistic. Tuna was unharmed. They had both survived the encounter. Neel Brighton was in the custody of the General Authorities. Several other ward members had arrived. As the conversation between the adults continued, Duke wore a carefree expression as he walked toward the temple exit without saying anything. Brother Godot approached Charlie before she could decide whether calling out to the dog would be acceptable.

"I guess Neel Brighton *did* visit me during his time as Secretary of the Interior to intercept that package. That probably should have raised a bigger red flag for me than it did at the time, but I was too busy trying to uncurse the sphinx and get it back to Bishop Liddell to worry about that. Even I can barely believe it just fell out of my pocket in the foyer," admitted Brother Godot as he went about rethinking his life. "I should have known your dad wasn't a murderer, Charlie."

"It's okay, Brother Godot. But Neel Brighton is kind of unhinged when working with archons. It could have happened to anyone," reassured Charlie. "Besides, how else would I have gotten such an adventure without finding that same sphinx in the foyer?"

Brother Godot smiled and walked away to talk to another ward member. Charlie had trouble finding a smile to return and instead overheard another conversation, picking her father's name out of it as her attention shifted.

"...wasn't you, Chuck. I'm sorry we had to detain you. Take Neel Brighton away to be detained instead, brethren," said a general authority.

"Thank you, Elder Cuarón, but I owe a lot to my daughter's help in this case," replied Charlie's father. "The gravity of your words will mean a great deal to the children of men."

"I would imagine your words mean a great deal for your little princess, too," added the General Authority. He turned to Charlie with a friendly smile. "We have great expectations for you to be obedient to the teachings of the church."

Charlie stared back at the man, long enough that he shifted his gaze and started to change the subject before she spoke up to say, "Are those the teachings that would honor our Heavenly Mother, too?"

Neel interrupted before anyone could answer the child's blunt question. "You've got nothing on me! It wasn't my fault."

"But you stole the plates," pointed out Chuck. "How is that not your fault?"

"I made a deal," admitted Neel. "Please, Elder Cuarón, I need to avoid jail time. I'm hoping to announce a run for office, and this could be terrible for me."

"With whom did you make a deal?" asked Elder Cuarón. "And don't tell me you can succeed only with your partner."

"No, it's nothing like that," insisted Neel. "I made a deal to steal artifacts from the museum with Coyote."

"But Coyote is a known trickster. Why would you make a deal with him?" questioned Vivi.

"While I am quite confident I would win my political bid, I didn't want to take any chances," rationalized Brother Brighton.

"It sounds like you just wanted some kind of justification," commented Vivi.

"Thank you, Elect Lady Liddell," remarked Elder Cuarón. "That will be all."

"It's quite the blemish. I wish you all luck in covering it up," replied Vivi.

"Where is Coyote now?" asked Tuna.

"Um, well, after Coyote tricked me, you'd have to swim up the nearby creek to find him," suggested Neel.

"Which creek is that?" inquired Charlie.

"He's probably half-way past Shinehah by now. You'd have to summon him all over again, and the ritual is quite complex," remarked Neel.

Everyone stared at him expectantly, waiting for further instructions.

"Well?" asked Chuck, when Neel said nothing. "What do we do?"

"You know, the ritual requires such precise timing with the wheel of the year and several days of uninterrupted prayer, and it just isn't feasible right now," offered Neel.

Those present were giving various looks of skepticism; Tuna judged him outright with the most skeptical face of all those present.

Sophia and Astanphaeus appeared in the Sacred Grove Temple with those gathered, enshrouding the temple room in a glorious light. Tuna closed her eyes, nuzzling into Charlie as the light localized to the archons. Each one appeared differently, as if woven from the very fabric of reality. Neither attempted to conjure a face this time.

"He conjured us," they offered in unison, as each voice sounded like a collective sigh of a world settling into slumber, both lulling and terrifying.

XIII

Monday School

Elder Cuarón grasped Brother Brighton's arm to prevent another escape.

Sophia and Astanphaeus fled the Sacred Grove Temple. Chuck immediately fled after the archons, with Charlie and Tuna in tow. In no time at all, they were running down the nearby Deseret Trail. The archons slipped inside a shack. As Bishop Liddell approached it, he stopped. The shack was covered in foreboding symbols and emanated evil. Charlie stopped, frightened by what would stop her father so suddenly. Tuna stared at it with her tail straight up and fluffed. The cat stood unmoving, other than releasing a low, threatening growl at the structure.

"We have to catch them, Charlie. They can destroy the world if they're allowed to run free here. I don't know why Sophia would allow it. She's usually so wise. What would drive her to work with Astanphaeus is unknown to me. We have to perform a banishing together if we've any hope of being protected in our pursuit from this point forward. Will you trust me?" asked her father.

"No," answered Charlie.

"No? Why not?" asked Chuck. "The fate of Deseret is at stake. What's wrong?"

"I just... you said the murder was my fault. But I cleared your name, anyway. And you didn't even apologize," said Charlie. "How can I trust you?"

Chuck had not taken the time to consider that consequence. He thought about his daughter's words, finding no answers. "I'm sorry. I don't know why I didn't think to apologize."

"I don't know, either. But I'll try to trust you anyway," decided Charlie.

Chuck took out a vial of consecrated oil and anointed himself and Charlie with some of it. After he put it away, she traced an upright pentagram in the same space as her father, following his lead. They sounded various musical notes as in tune to one another as a bass and soprano can be. Spheres of prismatic colors appeared at each point of the star. Tuna relaxed her pose as the evil energy dissipated from the area.

"Is it safe, Dad?" asked Charlie.

"I have faith we'll be safe. But I don't know," admitted her father.

Charlie nodded, reassured by Tuna and Chuck.

The trio continued to give chase into the shack, finding a ladder leading underground amid a pantheon of physical horrors remaining to decorate the innards of the shack. Charlie would later choose to refer to it as the Museum of Autopsy and avoided any further discussion on the matter. In the meantime, she passed through the shack, trying to forget it already.

"Tuna is unphased, because she is a cat. To Tuna, all places are the same," explained Tuna with the words sounding more like a monotonous repetition than anything with real meaning to the cat. She gave a distant stare down the tunnel ahead of the trio.

"I never want to visit the Museum of Autopsy again," noted Charlie.

They continued to chase the archons down the tunnel. It was easy to follow the archons, because a trail of sorts could be felt. Charlie pressed her father about the odd feeling, but it was all Chuck could do to describe it as *l'appel du vide*. Charlie had no knowledge of such a phrase existent in Deseret parlance. The trio took several turns at various intersections, never passing anything distinct enough from asymmetrical patches of concrete and rusting pipes to be noteworthy. Still, they followed the trail.

A patter of footsteps sounded ahead of the group, and the trio slowed to a stop to listen closer. A jangling of metal on metal sounded, as if a tag were hitting against the metal ring on a collar. From the darkness emerged a small dog.

"Duke!" exclaimed Tuna.

"Charlie! Tuna! Bishop Liddell! Fancy meetin' ya in the tunnels. Ya didn't nod off again, did ya Charlie?" asked Duke with concern.

"Afraid not, Duke. We had to perform a banishing to get in here through some creepy murderer's shack," explained Charlie.

"That sounds awfully dangerrrous, Charlie. How are ya handlin' it?" asked Duke, extending a paw to touch one of Charlie's blue and black striped shoes.

"Um, I think we're surviving?" answered Charlie, uncertain if those were the words the dog had hoped to hear.

"Looks like it! By the way, Father Sirius says you're a wizard, Charlie. Does that mean anythin' tah ya?" asked Duke, withdrawing his paw and looking with hope toward Charlie.

"I don't know, but Father Sirius's lack of exclusion in calling me a wizard certainly feels radical," mused Charlie.

"Your slang is lost on me, Earrrth child, but it's good tah see ya again. Good luck, Charlie," said Duke, walking away to a destination apparently best reached through the tunnels for a dog with Duke's inscrutable purposes.

The remaining run through the tunnels presented a trail somewhat more faintly than before, but still easy enough to follow. In no time at all, they had passed through the featureless tunnels and arrived back at the Sacred Grove Temple. Vivi entered the room to see what had caused the commotion.

"You're back! You'll never guess what happened after you left," said Vivi.

"Neel Brighton escaped?" asked Tuna.

"Well done, Tuna. Here, have a cat treat," said Vivi, producing a treat from a bag in her blue and red striped purse for the cat to devour before Charlie could object.

Charlie scoffed after watching the cat swallow the treat and questioned, "Where is Elder Cuarón? Where did Neel Brighton go this time?"

"Quick, follow me," implored Vivi, leading the way toward a closed door.

A strange energy intertwined with the feeling of *l'appel du vide* the group had been following to find the way here. The energy was vaguely familiar, yet somehow inverted. The feeling became almost overwhelming as Vivi opened the door.

Inside the room, Sophia and Astanphaeus appeared to be draining so much energy from Neel Brighton that a physical manifestation of the phenomenon was visible, linking ruby-tinged strands of energy between the archons and the man. It took several steps closer for Charlie to observe Neel was reading the golden plates, and a few additional steps in thinking to make the assumption these archons were draining Neel Brighton's spiritual energy.

"Quick, we have to do something!" declared Vivi, standing at Charlie's side.

"Hurry! We'll perform a banishing. There's no telling what the archons will do to this world if they harness the spiritual energy of not only a man, but also the golden plates," explained Chuck, joining his family.

Tuna stood in front of Charlie and faced her, with Neel Brighton at a distance behind the cat.

"Look out, Tuna," said Charlie. "I have to do this."

"As long as Tuna can have lap after," responded the cat with a huff before stepping aside for Charlie to help her parents.

Charlie, Vivi, and Chuck focused their efforts on minimizing the overall chaos unfolding within the temple. Time seemed to slow around Neel, trapping him in an eternity of spirit-draining torment as the stories upon the golden plates played out in his mind over and over again. The archons gorged themselves on the energy, feeding a small portion of their own powers back to Neel to keep him the same age forever and ever.

Tracing a pentagram before them, the trio manifested a star into existence. The archons and the man were bound within it. Tuna nuzzled herself against Charlie's leg.

"Tuna will stay with Charlie," resolved the cat.

"ABRACADABRA!" yelled Charlie with her parents.

Time stopped. All matter in the space within the borders of the star came to a halt. In Charlie's mind, it was only a few moments more before the banishing was complete and the archons were returned to their own realm. Perhaps the strength from the unit of the family factoring into the spell would be enough to keep the archons at bay.

Neel Brighton crumpled over the golden plates. Chuck ran to prop the man up, finding Neel Brighton breathing about as well as anyone else in this corrected position compared to the man's other recent moments.

Charlie stopped, refusing to do anything more. "I'm so done with this," Charlie muttered.

"We have to help Neel. What's wrong, Charlie?" asked Vivi.

"Then he can escape again and we can keep going around and around. Can we just not? I want to go home. The archons are banished, again. We won. Have Elder Cuarón help you, he seems to appreciate the direction you want to go," quipped Charlie.

"Charlie, that's not...." Vivi chose not to argue further with her daughter.

"I think what your mother was going to say is that was a bit insensitive, Charlie. I don't think you mean we should murder him now. Why don't you take Tuna home? There are some scripture verses I think you may find applicable to this situation. We'll go over them later," attempted Chuck.

"That isn't what I meant. Neel Brighton attacked me. For my part, I can no longer remain convinced one view is more true than the other," attempted Charlie.

Vivi and Chuck exchanged concerned glances.

"What do you mean by that, Charlie?" asked Vivi.

"Never mind," answered Charlie. "Come on, Tuna. Let's go home."

"But Charlie, don't you believe the church is true?" asked Chuck as his daughter walked away with Tuna in tow.

"I'm having my doubts," replied Charlie over her shoulder. She continued walking. Another saying about doubts went unsaid, but lingered in the back of their minds.

With Charlie headed back home, Chuck and Vivi saw to it Neel Brighton was hauled away to the hospital. With further insistence, the General Authorities handcuffed Brother Brighton once again, this time to the stretcher. Neel said nothing, having apparently spent all his resources in a last-ditch effort to meet his quota for trouble. His eyes looked less spirited than before the encounter with the archons.

At home, Charlie removed her black jacket with a few snaps of static audible while Tuna settled into Charlie's lap, unable to wait for the completion of the action. Charlie set the jacket aside, pondering all that had happened in her heart. Strange tunnels. Stranger entities. Dinosaurs. Ghosts. Mythical beings. And all because of a toy sphinx she had found in a foyer. A letter-sized envelope with her name on it slid under her door.

Outside the room, Chuck considered saying something to his daughter through the door. He walked away with something else on his mind, having already dismissed the thought.

Charlie looked at the envelope. Tuna looked at her, feeling Charlie's muscles tense as if she were going to get up and inspect the contents. Charlie relaxed and enjoyed being home with her cat, handing Tuna a treat from a bag tucked away at her bedside. Tuna ate it with some mix of greed and gratitude.

"But what if Charlie gets lost in another mystery, and can never give Tuna lap again?" asked Tuna, looking at Charlie with her big green eyes as if she had been deprived of all past and future joys.

"Why, Tuna, never having you on my lap again would be a mystery worth solving. You would practically be the cat in the box," answered Charlie.

Tuna looked around, finding herself very much outside of a box. "Tuna has not the luxury of a box," insisted the cat.

"No, meowface," began Charlie. "I meant to say, I could never lose you, because your paw prints are always well-worn on my heart. As long as I have the memory of you, you'll always be with me."

"Charlie knows what Tuna means," insisted the cat as she shifted her loafing on Charlie's lap with her whiskers ruffling.

"Yes, Tuna. I know what you mean," reassured Charlie. Her hand scratched behind Tuna's ears and the cat nuzzled into her. Time passed as the two of them enjoyed each other's company. At last, Tuna let out a sigh and relaxed, purring herself to sleep on Charlie's lap. Charlie pondered the future in her heart as she drifted off to sleep, too.

Acknowledgement

This work would not have been possible without the inspiration of Ben Mack, Robert Anton Wilson, Kerry Shirts, Dan Vogel, Bill Reel, RFM, The Amazing Maven, Rebecca Biblioteca, Margaret & Paul Toscano, Fred Silverman, Trent Harris, S. William Snider, Dr. Justin Sledge, Joseph Smith, Aleister Crowley, Lewis Carroll, Peter Carroll, Ralph Tegtmeier, Terence McKenna, Alan Watts, Doug Wildey, William Hanna, Joseph Barbera, Joe Ruby, Ken Spears, and the various voluminous volumes of work produced by those mentioned and those adjacent to those aforementioned but otherwise remaining unmentioned here. Thank you all.